THE MAN WHO STOLE THE MONA LISA

THE MAN WHO STOLE THE MONA LISA

MARTIN PAGE

PANTHEON BOOKS, NEW YORK

For Matthew

I am particularly grateful to Stephen Price-Jones of the Cour-
tauld Institute of Fine Art for his expertise on forgery, to the late
Elmyr de Hory for his less academic advice on the same subject,
to Gill Page for her guidance in the South American sequence, to
Sarah Crowley for her research into the Italian episode, to the
librarians of the Centre Pompidou, Paris, the British Newspaper
Library and the Baker Library, Hanover, New Hampshire, to the
Paris Police for not arresting us while we were examining and
photographing the Louvre's ventilation system, to Jane Mays for
her almost always good-tempered hard work during the early
stages of the novel and, above all, to Catherine.

Libarary of Congress Cataloging in Publication Data

Page, Martin, 1938–
The man who stole the Mona Lisa.

I. Title.
PR6066.A34M3   1984   823'.914   84-42699
ISBN 0-394-53283-X
0-394-74098-X (pbk)

Manufactured in the United States of America
First Paperback Edition

1909

The collar of John Pierpont Morgan's sable coat was raised around his stout neck. The rim of his fur-lined top hat pressed against his protruding ears. Refusing the supporting arm of his footman, he began to walk alone down the steps from his pink marble palace to Madison Avenue. A third of the way down, he failed in his resolve to keep his mind off the subject of the human race, and his eyes firmly fixed on the open door of his motor carriage.

Though rarely publicised in advance, his exits and entrances more rarely went unnoticed. Through November's sleet, he saw in the crowd on the sidewalk the Jew, as old as himself, who kept daily vigil. Suspended from a piece of string around his neck was his placard. It bore a photograph of Morgan beneath the headline: 'THE FACE OF CAPITALISM!'

Morgan sometimes pondered whether the socialists grasped the profundity of their propaganda against him. If he were not so ugly, he would not have devoted his life to compensating for it. He would not have become so rich, and the industrial development of America would have been retarded by perhaps half a century.

Tonight, boarding his carriage, he had the sensation — indeed a conviction, however unprovable — that standing beside the old Jew was a younger man, watching him with neither ideological nor casual intensity. Morgan's vision was blurred by age and weather; and he could not see whether the features matched those of the description supplied to him by the Pinkerton Detective Agency.

Once under way to Grand Central Station, he began to breathe more quietly. He enjoyed being driven through

Manhattan, especially after dark. Only a decade ago, it had seemed a drab provincial town, particularly when compared with his native London: a squat, brownstone mass of storefronts and tenements, its monotony broken by little but austere, brownstone churches. The broad avenues were potholed and littered with horse manure, which iced obscenely in winter and stank in summer. Now, Morgan saw in the freezing mist outside elegantly soaring skyscrapers, some already completed, built of Morgan steel and mortgaged to the Morgan bank. He passed new department stores, stocked with luxury goods brought from the Old World in Morgan ships. The grocery shops were crammed with unseasonal foods from warmer climates, harvested by Morgan agricultural machines and freighted on Morgan railroads. The department stores' pre-Christmas window displays glistened, as did the streets and avenues, with electricity generated from Morgan coal by the Morgan power company.

In the evening rush-hour through which Morgan's chauffeur steered, horse-drawn vehicles were now well-outnumbered by motorised ones. They were less grand than Morgan's carriage; but they had been manufactured from Morgan metals, and their purchase by individuals financed by Morgan eight per cent loans. Instead of fouling the roadways, their gaseous excreta blended with the atmosphere, adding to its winter sparkle. For how much longer could Boston proclaim itself the World Capital of Progress, the Hub of the Universe?

The chauffeur turned into 23rd Street. The wind suddenly died away, and the sleet thickened. Morgan could see little outside but the myopic yellow glow of Morgan patent arc-lamps. The outright purchase of the invention from Edison had proved as profitable and pleasing to the eye as it had been inexpensive. He switched on his interior light, took from his pocket the crumpled Commercial Company cablegram, and read it again.

'BE READY TO RECEIVE OUR MISTER FOSTER ON BOARD YOUR RAILROAD CAR AT ALBANY NNNYYY 10 REPEAT 10 AYEM NOVEMBER 22 REPEAT 22 TRULY YOURS LONDON ART LTD.'

Could, by some mischance, London Art Ltd really exist? Employ a representative called Foster? But if the sender was Worth, and if he had felt the need for an alias, why had he despatched the message so unprivately, through a Morgan-owned telegraph office four blocks down Madison Avenue from the Morgan mansion? Morgan's mind cleared. The sender was making it easy for Morgan to obtain a description of him and compare it with Pinkerton's.

But if it was Worth, how could he know — or at least presume — that in order to meet him, John Pierpoint Morgan would cancel engagements at short notice; that he would pretend a sudden wish to inspect the headquarters of the Albany and Susquehanna Railroad; that he would travel 150 miles overnight into the bleakness of upstate New York — quite possibly to be made a fool of? From the evidence, Worth himself was, or until very recently had been, in Manhattan.

He had known of Worth's existence for only two weeks. Worth seemed to know him intimately. Morgan shut his eyes to pray. It had taken him many years to perceive God through his cloud of resentment. Even now, they were not fond of one another, but exchanged grudging respect.

O Lord, You have given me more wealth than any man before me. And more fame than many emperors and tsars. I do not know why You still torment me with my ugliness. Why did You give me a beautiful wife, but cripple her with poliomyelitis and embitter her towards me? Mistresses who overcame their repellence only because of my wealth? I'm eighty-one, Lord. Soon, You will take me from this world. Send Worth to me in Albany tomorrow. Guide him to accept my commission. Grant me the time to see it achieved. Then I shall come willingly to You — but not before.

He opened his eyes again. On his left, a horse-drawn cab suddenly accelerated and then swerved diagonally in front of his motor carriage. The horse slipped on the wet cobbles, cried out, and fell. The chauffeur braked and Morgan heard from behind him traffic collide and stop. The cab's passenger, an agile man, slammed its door shut behind him and walked rapidly into the enveloping mist.

The chauffeur, returning from his investigations, reported, 'The police say it will take a half-hour to fetch hoisting tackle, to raise the horse.'

'Find out how much the horse costs. Pay the cabbie. Shoot the horse with your revolver. Then have it dragged clear, on to the sidewalk.'

The chauffeur hesitated. Morgan could not recall his name. He glared at him through his black, bulging eyes. In under three minutes, he heard two shots. In less than another five, the motor carriage was moving again, followed by the rest of the traffic.

Morgan leant back, wondering whether he had just outwitted God, or Worth.

So as to catch the earliest possible glimpse of his visitor, John Pierpont Morgan defied medical advice. You could pay a doctor to prod, probe and lecture you any day. Within the next few minutes, he would be exorcising the spirit that had come to haunt him over the past two weeks, and see it to be a mere mortal with a pricetag.

To and fro through the fresh, bright upstate morning, he paced the platform of Albany Central — slowly as he faced the station's entrance, then rapidly with his back to it on the return journey.

The ten o'clock local left for Shenectady and Amsterdam. The station became silent, but for the hissing steam from Morgan's own locomotive and the crunching of his own feet on the new snow. In the icy breeze, his nose — the vast, reddish-purple protuberance with which God had cursed or perhaps blessed him from birth, and later embellished with uncurable boils — began to ache. As he boarded his car, a wave of self-pity rose in his groin, passed through his stomach and progressed up his spine.

In the saloon, he sat himself in a Louis XV armchair (a gift from a French prime minister whose name now eluded him) before the coal-fire burning in the Florentine grate. He lit a black stumpy cigar and would have ordered brandy if his digestion could have taken it. He picked up the Pinkerton Detective Agency's inch-thick dossier on Worth, A. (Real Name Untraced), whose contents he already knew. Then, he heard a collision of shoe-leather on the iron steps, and a voice in the vestibule — a baritone, Bostonian voice — announcing its owner to be Mr Foster.

It took the visitor what seemed to Morgan an unduly long time to discard his coat, hat, gloves and overshoes. When he entered the saloon, he immediately so absorbed himself in its furnishings and embellishments that he might not have noticed its owner's presence.

He seemed several inches taller, years younger and more imposing than Pinkerton's description allowed. He was certainly better-looking than Morgan had believed Jews could be. His nose did not bulge, nor did his eyes protrude, nor were his lips meaty. Here was a craggy, hard-living but clear-skinned face with gentle eyes, an elegantly trimmed crop of straight, brown hair and a darker brown Mark Twain moustache, probably false. Morgan felt only passing envy. *Blessed are the ugly and determined, for they acquire the wealth and power to command the handsome and clever*.

It was the clothing that aroused Morgan's suspicion: a chain-store suit, also brown but with imitation-silver stripes. Beneath the Celluloid collar was an art-silk Dartmouth College necktie, which no alumnus would be seen wearing, fixed with a false-diamond pin. It was as though he had re-fitted himself at J.C. Penney on his way to the station.

The visitor surveyed the Burmese teak panelling and the Syrian tiled ceiling. He inspected the Gobelins tapestry of St Amelia and the Milkmaids, the Venetian chandeliers and the Manchurian rugs. He glanced at Fra Angelica's altar-triptych, and the carved marble fire-surround attributed to Michelangelo. He looked towards Morgan.

'It's still more remarkable than they say. Not your face, I mean, this car. It was considerate of you to bring it up here, to allow me to see it.'

'You had Morgan travel all this way so you could look around my car?'

'I travel much, sometimes in reasonable comfort, but never before on board a private railroad car.'

It was a display of impertinence that Morgan's failing memory thought to be unprecedented.

The visitor helped himself to one of Morgan's cigars and sat down. 'If you'll have the engineer start back for New York City, I'll be at your disposal for as much of the journey as you wish.'

The man's unexplained lateness was about to lose Morgan's through-signalling priority. He had perhaps two minutes more to decide whether he was the impostor himself, or one hired and trained by him — whether to keep him on board or throw him off.

'Where were you last night?'

'I'd thought the people you've had following me would have told you. I ate early at Krugmayer's. I don't know whether you've ever tried to eat the dinners your railroad serves fare-paying passengers . . .'

'Then?'

'I waited outside your *palazzo* to check that you left it. I knew this car had been hitched to the nine o'clock Great Lakes Limited, and had a ticket for the Pullman. But it could have been a Pinkerton trap. Then, bad weather put my timing out on the way to the station. So I paid a cabbie to cut you off, to have the train held up for you while I caught it.'

Morgan's eyelids began to close.

'Sir, there is a warrant out for my arrest in Albany, and I should appreciate our leaving this town.'

The train raced south at over thirty miles an hour. It passed through snow-covered hills and a village of white clapboard houses, clustered around a red-brick water-mill. Worth smoked the cigar and drank Bristol sherry. He sat at the window at right angles to Morgan, whose hand was resting on the cardboard cover of the dossier.

'Mr Worth.' Morgan stopped himself and started again. 'Now I accept you to be Adam Worth, why can I still not recognise you from the descriptions I have of you?'

'That's a personal question. This is a business meeting.'

'If I'm to do business with you . . .'

'I have a plastic face. I can change it at will.'

'Change it.'

Worth shook his head. 'Were it so simply achieved, I would slip without conscious control from one appearance to another, and I'd be employed in a Barnum and Bailey sideshow. I am not a circus freak, Mr Morgan, but an artist. After years of practice, it takes up to two hours of concentration to compose and fix my features. Today's face is a new one, created for this meeting, which is why I was a few minutes late.'

'Your moustache?'

'Tug it for yourself. I am not amateur. That's partly why I had to keep you waiting two weeks, after our mutual friend Pinkerton said you wanted this meeting.'

Mutual friend? Morgan forbade himself indulgence in thoughts about conspiracies against him. His thumb slipped familiarly into the dossier. 'It's not just a question of today's face, Mr Worth. Read this for yourself.'

'I have.'

Morgan's thick black eyebrows moved towards one another, almost converging in the dip above his nose. 'I hope you're lying, Mr Worth. Not even my private secretary knows this dossier exists. I paid Pinkerton five thousand dollars to investigate you himself, then to lock himself in a hotel room, at my further expense, and have his meals sent in while he wrote you up. He delivered his report to me personally, and it hasn't been outside my sight since.'

'The Balmoral Hotel, White Plains, room 206.' Worth sipped his sherry. 'Mr Pinkerton values your custom. It has made his previously modest firm the US Steel or United Fruit Company of detective agencies. So he asked me to stay in room 207, which has an inter-communicating door, in return for cancelling the fees I owed him as a client.'

Morgan, craving hard liquor, swallowed some seltzer. His train, having lost its priority while his visitor was arranging his face, was now halted by the signal north of Bethlehem. 'It says you robbed my bank in Boston. You forged my letters of credit in Belgium. You stole jewellery I had given a lady acquaintance in New York. Having disguised yourself for the purpose, you cheated me at baccarat in London. In Cannes, you pirated my steam-yacht for eight days, ostensibly for your honeymoon. You stole from my London dealers, the night I agreed to buy it, Gainsborough's *Duchess of Devonshire*, the finest portrait of a woman ever painted by an English artist. You then retained my detective agency to act for you, in ransoming it back. Now you sit in my car, as though it were already yours.' Morgan was finding it ever-harder to conceal his admiration. 'And say you have corrupted Mr Pinkerton himself into deceiving me. Are you comfortable to be my guest, sir?'

'Please don't take it personally. It was my *curriculum vitae*. I did no more than amend some minor flaws and fill out some sections where Mr Pinkerton's own knowledge was lacking.'

The train began to move again. '*Curriculum vitae*? You didn't even tell him your name.'

'Obviously I'd have done so, if I knew it. When my family arrived here, the immigration officer allocated us the surname "Litvak", along with two hundred others on the same boat. Later, I asked my parents for our real name. They said Litvak had been specially chosen for us by the US Government and was good enough.'

'It's happened to hundreds of thousands of others. How did it turn you against me?'

They were passing a Lutheran chapel. Its Wayside Pulpit billboard, facing the track, proclaimed: 'THOU SHALT NOT STEAL.' Someone had added in bold, black paint strokes: 'MORGAN — 8% INTEREST'.

'Against you? It's a tribute.'

Was he, after all, just another smart-arse Jew trying to flim-flam him? 'Go on, Mr Worth.'

'When I entered the criminal world, I soon noted two factors about it. First, its members tended to work in debilitating competition against one another. Second, they looked on profits as spending money, and so denied themselves the adequate capital base they required for success. I compared this with the Morgan approach.'

The car jolted — over-compacted ice? An iron divot left on the track by a disaffected railroad employee? The paintings and tapestries, even the porcelain figurines on the mantel were so well secured they did not shudder.

Morgan watched Worth's glass fall sideways, spreading a yellow stain over the damask tablecover. 'You've spilt your drink, Mr Worth. Are you a nervous man?'

Worth considered the question for some moments and replied, 'Not unusually so, sir, for someone in your presence. I'd appreciate it if you'd have your servant bring me another.'

Morgan sensed an irritation in himself reminiscent of that he had felt towards the studied impassivity of the psychiatrist he'd once hired to cure his wife of her distaste for him. 'What's this "Morgan approach"?'

'You seem to have studied the theories of Dr Karl Marx more carefully than I, despite my late father's urgings, and applied them with remarkable effect. Money is capital, and capital the glue which can bind business rivals together and so stop them engaging in wasteful competition. Thus they're freed to pursue maximum profit, which in turn becomes more capital. It could never be made to work in a backward country like the Russian Empire, where I was born. But you made it a powerful force in the lives of Americans.'

Morgan, puzzled, peered through the window and saw a brown cow-barn. A boy, laughing, ran from it, without coat or hat across the snow.

'Mr Worth, Marx urges the confiscation of capital from those of us who manipulate it for the common good.'

An old man in brown dungarees brandishing a snow-shoe came out of the barn and began to chase the boy. Worth's composure or insolence was remarkable. 'Only when the monopolies have been created by men like you. That won't be in my lifetime. Perhaps in your grandchildren's.'

The boy had tripped on a hemlock bush and was no longer laughing. As he struggled to get back on his feet, the old man caught up with him and began to beat his backside.

'You seem offended, sir,' said Worth. 'Please don't think I under-estimate your achievements. US Steel, International

Harvester, Consolidated Edison and the rest are impressive progress towards the goal of a just society. That's why I set out to emulate you in my own field.'

Morgan turned back to his guest. 'You overlook the fundamental moral difference between us. You are a Jew. I am an Episcopalian. Almost everything I have done has been within the law.'

Worth was the first Jew Morgan could recall meeting who did not rise to catch his tongue on the baited hook.

'If the criminal community had the same power as you to make and change laws, they would keep within them too. It was most principled of you to shut down your establishment in England, when the Government introduced death duties.'

Hadn't Pinkerton briefed him? Morgan became more aware of the ache in the back of his neck.

'As my guest, Mr Worth, I forbid you from mentioning death again.'

'I am speaking of life, and would like more sherry. I applied your principles to my own field. I organised a series of minor thefts — nothing large enough to arouse serious attention of the police. Instead of splitting the proceeds, I distributed only one fifth of them in dividends, and deposited the remainder with your bank in Bayton. Soon, I had enough to buy the lease on the barber's shop next door to your bank and tunnel through into your vault. I've not looked back since. You'd launched my career.'

'Which has been almost entirely at my expense.'

'It would hardly have been fair if it had been anyone else's. I was applying your philosophy.'

'Why do you admit all this so freely?'

'I do so only to you. I thought you had a need for my services and wished to check my credentials.'

'Are you curious about what that need might be?'

'I imagine you want me to steal the Mona Lisa from the Louvre in Paris.'

Morgan felt a pimple above his left nostril about to burst. Involuntarily, he raised his hand to squeeze it between his thumb and forefinger. His guest neither averted his eyes nor registered disgust. Had Pinkerton gleaned some hint, and passed it on? Not possible. He wiped the pus on to his handkerchief. 'How in hell did you figure that out?'

'Otherwise, John Pierpont Morgan would hardly go to such inconvenience, and risk such potential embarrassment, to meet the man with the reputation of the world's most skilled thief. Why else would you do that, except to have me steal the world's most valuable object?'

'But why should I want it so much?'

'That is your private affair. I assume partly because you are the world's greatest art collector, trying to turn New York into the finest treasure-house on earth. The French Government refused to sell it to you. You intend teaching them a lesson: if you can't have it, nobody shall. Also because your private collection of portraits of beautiful women, though large, remains second rate without it.'

It was as though Worth had perceived his motives more clearly than he had done himself.

'Were that correct, how would you convince me you could do it?'

'You could hardly expect me to disclose the methods I would use. Besides, such knowledge would cause you only unnecessary worry.'

'How many people would you need?'

'Myself.' Worth took another cigar. 'This is not arrogance. Among the unique problems of stealing the Mona Lisa is the present Prefect of Paris, Monsieur Louis Lepine. He is one of Europe's few thinking policemen, possibly the only one. If I understand his recent monograph on criminal behaviour correctly — and I am reasonably fluent in French — he asserts it is a myth that criminality is the preserve of a specific social class. It is rather a mental disposition universal to human nature. It is also, as a trait, inherently lacking in originality.

'A thief — whether stealing an apple from his neighbour's garden, or a wagon-load of Morgan bullion — instinctively applies his one approach to such a challenge every time. Try as he may to change it, all he achieves is a little dressing up. The fundamentals are beyond his power to alter.

'As each human being is unique, it follows that a thief leaves what Lepine calls his "mental imprint" at the scene of every crime he commits. He may leave no fingerprints or other physical traces. There may be no witnesses. But by discerning the "mental imprint", a detective can unerringly trace the crime back to the mind's owner. It's not just a theory that puts Scotland Yard and our own FBI, by comparison, on the intellectual level of an elementary school. It works.'

Morgan opened Pinkerton's dossier at a page marked with a yellow strip of silk, and read again: '*Much of the problem in assessing Worth's character is his capacity for "total" impersonation. In my observation his abilities, as well as the immorality of his intentions in this matter, far exceed those of any professional stage actor. By whatever combination of intellectual and spiritual powers, he creates in even a close observer not merely a consistently false and complete personality and facial expression, but even the impression of a variable physique.*'

Morgan looked up at Worth. 'Stand up, beside the table.'

As Worth did so, he continued, 'Any professional who has acquired sufficient skill to work with me on rescuing the Mona Lisa inevitably also has his "mental imprint" known to Lepine. They'd be picked up before we got the painting to Cherbourg.'

'But he surely has yours too, Mr Worth. Will you please remove your shoes?'

Worth did not bend to untie his laces. He levered his right toe-cap against his left heel and then reversed the procedure. Straightening himself again, he seemed to Morgan to have become a little taller in the process. It was a simple enough trick — so long as one had had the foresight to keep one's spine curved all the while before.

'If I may conclude, Mr Morgan, I intend, sir, to prove Lepine wrong.'

Morgan retired to the lavatory, not primarily to relieve himself, but to think. The rational part of his mind seemed to have blanked out. He returned to the saloon.

'How much will you charge?'

'Five million dollars.' Morgan saw him lower his cigar to the ashtray, to steady himself. 'One million in advance. One when the theft has been achieved. Three on delivery.'

It was five times more than Morgan had anticipated. 'That's robbery,' he said.

Worth breathed deeply. 'It's what you offered the French Government for the painting. To pay any less would be immoral.'

Morgan opened his eyes wide and stared at his guest. 'Mr Worth, I am going to tell you something I have never told any man before. When I was very young, my mother read me the story of Beauty and the Beast. It's a fine tale of a good and beautiful girl's love for a creature of grotesque appearance, but who had a pure heart. When my mother finished reading it, she did not kiss me goodnight. She then sent me to live abroad in the care of a governess.'

'It's inexpedient to dwell on such memories,' Worth replied coldly.

'Don't dare interrupt. My wife refused to marry me until she became a cripple and had no option because her parents couldn't afford to keep her. I carried her to the altar, and she's detested me ever since. As for female acquaintances. . . . Mr Worth, the point is, the moment I first looked at the Mona Lisa in the Louvre all those years ago, I saw she'd been misrepresented. The key to her isn't the smile, so much as the eyes. You can walk back and forth in front of her countless times, and those approving, loving eyes follow you every moment. Why, a man could stand in front of her and. . . . A man could do anything in front of her. I intend to die in front of her.'

He had startled Worth into silence. 'How do you want the first million?'

'Nine equal letters of credit drawn on banks other than your own. The remaining hundred thousand in English gold sovereigns.'

'A man who presents a letter of credit in France for a hundred thousand dollars attracts unwelcome attention.'

'I don't believe in trying to conceal my presence when travelling on business. To do so would arouse the strongest suspicion towards me.'

Worth drained his sherry and stubbed out his cigar. 'If you will have this train stop at the next station, which I think to be Poughkeepsie, I shall leave you, and contact you when I am ready. In the meantime, I should be grateful for an advance of ten dollars, so that I may complete my journey by public transport.'

'*Dear Pinkerton*, [Morgan wrote], *I command your agency to follow and observe the man known as Adam Worth wherever he goes, until further notice. You will not do this yourself but assign members of your staff. You will forward me reports written in their own hands weekly or more frequently if advisable. At no time are you yourself to communicate with so-called Worth, or report on his activities to any authority but myself. . . .*'

1911

It is a privilege given to few men — that is, those whose bodies and souls are still united — to attend their own funerals. For his, Adam Worth had hired a Rolls Royce Silver Ghost and the only black-skinned chauffeur in London, a Bahamian, willing to rent out the dignity of his hue to such an occasion.

Before the cortege started for Highgate Cemetery, he had the chauffeur wait fifty yards down Liverpool Road from what had been his English residence, so as not to intrude upon the widow's grief. Not that she had arranged much in the way of obsequies for his official quietus: an open two-horse hearse and one four-wheeler for the mourners. It was at least more than the corpse in the coffin would have received on his own account.

Fleet Street's tribute was gratifying. Perhaps thirty reporters and photographers were across the road in carriages and cars and on bicycles. Of his four wives, he would have preferred to have widowed Hannah in Brooklyn. But Margaret was English; and in London he had been more celebrated as a thief than in New York. Here, even a series of novelettes had been published about him, in which he was re-christened Raffles and transformed — to cater to patriotic pride — into an upper-class Englishman. London was from where the news of his death and burial would reach the world, J.P. Morgan and Louis Lepine.

Margaret came out of the house, her face thickly veiled. As the cortege began to move, it was joined from a side-street by a Scotland Yard car and another whose identity Worth could not perceive. Beside him, in the back of the Rolls, his new bride Angelica began to weep. In his meditations, he had forgotten her presence.

'There's no need to cry,' he said gently. 'You never even met him.'

He put his arm around her shoulder and pressed his palm against a young, firm breast beneath the tight bodice of her crepon mourning dress. He felt her nipple harden, a little too readily in the solemn circumstances.

She swept back her veil and looked up at him through oval, chocolate-brown, tearful eyes. 'Isn't it what I'm supposed to do? We always did in funeral processions back home.'

'Whatever makes you comfortable.' Angelica was exceeding his expectations in her supporting role of wife to the Anglo-South American gentleman he had decided to become.

Never before had he devoted himself so carefully to devising a new persona. So far, it had cost over $90,000 of Morgan's money, a year of his own time and almost his life.

He had collected the English gold sovereigns from Morgan's agent in New Orleans. That same afternoon, he purchased a cabin-class passage to Rio de Janeiro, on a ship leaving at high tide that night. A few minutes later, a man who had followed him into the Delta Steamship office, and who effused the stolidity of a Pinkerton agent, bought another one.

They travelled together, in different cabins and eating at different tables. The second evening out, at the bar, Worth took up a position next to where the Pinkerton man was standing, staring silently into his watered Southern Comfort. The latter signed for his drink and took it to an armchair in the corner.

It was raining in Rio. Worth checked into the Grand Hotel Ingles and paid at the desk for three nights' accommodation. While the Pinkerton agent was doing likewise, he went with his luggage through the staff exit which he found behind the elevators.

At the Nicaraguan consular office on the dockside, he bought for 30,000 *escudos* a passport in the name of George Cunningham, Minerals Prospector, born in Managua, back-dated by four years. As his mother had always professed uncertainty as to the year of his birth, he awarded himself the age of forty-six. He dropped his American passport into a rushing storm drain which would carry it out to sea where anyone who found it could make of it, or make use of it, as they wished. Less than two hours later he was on board a coastal freighter, bound for Belem, at the mouth of the Amazon. From there, he took the paddle-steamer for the tedious, four-day journey almost 600 miles up the wide river to Manaus.

The paddle-steamers went no further, for this was where what the Brazilians termed 'civilisation' ended. It was an opulent town, whose white residents appeared to be divided between those who were millionaires and those who were resolved on becoming so by stripping the surrounding jungle of its rubber and its hardwoods, its gems and its elusive, precious ores. For the time being, Worth denied himself the pleasures of the opera house and the casino, of promenading the boulevard and strolling in the botanical gardens. Eschewing, as well, the comforts of the Hotel Tropicale, he installed himself in a water-front rooming house, with rats running beneath the floor-boards. The only excursions he permitted himself were to assemble his kit of prospecting equipment and stores.

The landlord told him of a rubber trader's steam-launch going up river to Tefe. Worth bought deck space. The boat trudged slowly against the current, stopping three or four times a day at small clearings where surly Indians waited to trade latex for rum and axes. Twice daily, the boat's cook served chunks of Amazon turtle, stewed in brown river water in a large pail. A dull ache established itself in Worth's stomach. He began to fast, but the ache developed into stabbing pain. His bowels felt as though they were about to collapse under the strain of his dysentery; and he had the sensation that his skin was being scalded. He remembered the captain saying *fiebre negra*, black fever, and being carried ashore by two of the half-caste crew.

He had been taken to a mission. Two white Fathers tried to force him to drink intolerable quantities of boiled water, laced with sugar, salt and essence of opium, for days and nights he could not count, in a small wooden room. Time after time, he brought it up. Time after time, they brought him more. Father

James would say, 'You're doing better. You're a good patient.'

Father Horthy would add, 'Stop being so damned stubborn. I *order* you to hold it down.'

Before he could reply, the cup was being forced between his lips again.

One Sunday — he did not know how many had passed since his arrival — Father James declared him fit enough to attend mass.

'I am not a Catholic.'

'Clearly not,' said Father Horthy. 'We ask you to attend to set an example to natives.'

The chapel had no walls, but a roof of dried, interwoven jungle shrubs. Beneath were wooden benches, upon which sat a congregation of over three hundred, all of them men. Father James officiated, reciting Latin as incomprehensible to the Indians as it was to Worth. The former were at least knowledgeable as to when to stand, sit and kneel, and Worth followed their movements. Father James ate a wafer, drank wine and served Father Horthy. There were no other communicants. After the final prayer, the Indians rose quickly and went outside. They silently helped themselves with their hands to the contents of a large cauldron of lukewarm cassava and left.

For his own meal, Worth sat with the priests at table for the first time. 'Why do you have only male converts?'

'As yet, we have no converts,' said Father James.

'And won't for a long time,' said Father Horthy. 'They come for the free lunch. If they allowed their women to attend too, they think there'd be that much less food to go round.'

'Why don't you tell them otherwise?'

'We did, but they couldn't believe it. The proposition is too far from their terms of reference,' said Father James. 'It takes them a lot of effort to obtain food. They look after their girls and women tolerably well through pregnancy, in the hope of boy children. But if a woman's male babies die, which is often, or she gives birth to a succession of girls, which is almost as common, she has to fend for herself. In any event, when her child-bearing capacity is over — and the menopause occurs around the mid-thirties — the woman has a choice: she can either go out and collect food for the men and eat the leftovers herself, or she's thrown out of the village to survive or starve alone.'

Father Horthy said: 'If we broke their rules, they'd throw us out.'

During his convalescence, Worth questioned them about the locality. He was about three hundred miles up-river from Manaus. There was a village called Caori which would suit him, from the priests' description of it: a small, comparatively prosperous Indian settlement on the San Madre tributary, and the nearest white man — a recluse German latex-converter, who had dedicated his life to experiments to make rubber edible — a week's canoeing away. Before he felt quite fit enough, he chartered three dug-outs with paddlemen, one for himself, the others for his equipment and stores. The priests refused Worth's offer of money. Father James said, 'We have learnt from nursing you. It is enough.'

Worth stared at him warily though his still dulled eyes.

Father Horthy said, 'We have never before treated a European with black fever who survived in our care.'

'All the more reason that I should pay you.'

'No,' said Father Horthy. 'Over thirty years ago, I learnt at the tropical medicine institute that the fever affects whites far more severely than it does the natives. I've wondered ever since what was God's purpose in this, coming as we do as His civilising missionaries.'

Worth began to relax a little. A belated moral insight unintentionally given, that you interfered in other people's lives to your own detriment, was harmless enough repayment.

'Our debt to you is this,' said Father Horthy. 'When in delirium from, say, malaria or yellow fever, the European, when he speaks at all, meanders uncontrollably. In his semi-consciousness, it is as though he is unable to hear, and so he cannot converse. In your black-fever delirium, you were often aware of what was being said to you and able to respond with some coherence, although apparently unaware that you were doing so.'

'It is like a truth drug,' said Father James. 'A remarkable aid to confession. Specially valuable, given the often fatal nature of the disease.'

'What did I confess?' Worth was as curious as he was alarmed.

'A remarkable story,' said Father James. 'As a non-Catholic, you may not entirely trust in confessional secrecy; and, according to our rules, we are not bound by it in your case. But it is our vocation to die here. You're probably the last European we shall ever meet. The only person to whom we write is our Superior in Antwerp, who would not be interested. So your secret is safe enough with us.'

So long as Pinkerton's man did not pick up the trail. 'Can the fever recur?'

'We only have textbook knowledge of survivors,' said Father Horthy. 'If they are right, you have little cause to worry. You have come through the major attack, and your blood should have developed an immunity to future ones. The worst you should suffer are occasional bouts of deliria. Nothing alarming — a day, a couple of days, so long as you dose yourself with quinine.'

'Would these bouts cease if I went back to Europe?'

Father Horthy smiled as at a catechist who was at last on the verge of grasping an elusive theological point. 'The tendency is now in your body, no matter to where you transport it. If you choose not to alter your intentions for the future, and wish to continue to keep them private, our best advice is this: before a bout takes you over, be careful to select the company in which you are to suffer it as well as you did this time.'

'The safest people,' Father James added, 'are those who are both stupid and unable to speak English, but one or other would probably suffice in an emergency.'

'How much advance warning will I be able to feel?'

'That obviously depends upon your own self-awareness. The textbooks say anything from a week to under half an hour.'

At first sight, Caori met his requirements. No one greeted him at the landing place, and he walked up the narrow path the senior paddleman had pointed out to him before departing down-river. The village was without mission or trading post as the priests had said. Its only structures were unwalled huts built of wooden staves and palm frond roofs. While it was far from deserted, it might as well have been so in its reception. Unchallenged by the Indians as he wandered around, Worth could not even catch them in the act of looking at him. In the Upper Amazon, he had been taught at the mission, it is an unwise visitor who makes the first social move. He selected a site just outside the settlement, carried his baggage from the riverbank himself, and pitched his tent. He unpacked axes, necklaces and flagons of cactus rum. He arranged them in a pyramidal display at the tent's entrance. He unfolded his camp chair and sat, his Winchester repeating rifle placed prominently across his knees, and waited.

Naked children gave way to curiosity first, towards dusk. They stared at him through the undergrowth and giggled. Very slowly, he stood up. They ran away.

On the morning of the third day, a thin, elderly woman — forty years of age or more — approached meekly. When she was within two paces of him, she slowly put her hand behind her back and pulled a metal-bladed knife from beneath her waist-string that supported her pubic covering of dried leaves. She levelled the knife horizontally at his throat while, with her left hand, she reached down to pick up a flagon of cactus rum.

Worth returned her stare and while she was thus distracted, he kicked her with his booted foot just below her right knee-cap. He rose quickly, caught her in the small of her back as she toppled. With his free hand he pressed her hard between her breasts, turning her over in an involuntary somersault. Then he let her drop to the ground, front down.

She began to recover her breath. He picked up her knife and snapped it in two while she watched. He then placed a flagon in each of her hands and sat down again. Grasping them, she got to her feet and ran away.

Next day, a man came to the tent. He had in one hand a small, feathered dart with a darkened tip, and in his other an emptied flagon. Worth picked up a full one, and offered it. The man beckoned.

He was led to a muddy clearing surrounded by huts. In its centre an old man squatted alone, a crumpled white feather stuck in his hair. The escort knelt in the mud, so Worth did likewise. He extended the full flagon towards the chief with his right arm, as the White Fathers had advised. The chief took it but had trouble removing the cork. The escort pulled it with his teeth, and handed the flagon back.

The chief took a large swallow, coughed, and put the flagon on the ground. Then he raised his hand, four fingers and a thumb outstretched. Worth, equally silently, went back to his camp and returned with five more flagons.

The social ice broken, by means of stick drawings in the mud Worth commissioned the Indians to help him build a reasonably rain-proof cabin with the novel luxuries of a shingled roof, walls and — most puzzling of all to the natives — a wood-plank floor. They departed with the goods he presented them, and paid him no further attention.

In his cabin, Worth sat out the monsoon season. He ate Maggi concentrated soup cubes and canned tongue, beef and asparagus. He eked out his supply of quinine and smoked Monte Christo cigars. With the rain pounding on the roof, and dripping through it in places, he failed in his efforts to give his mind to his reading matter: an abridged, one-volume, traveller's edition of Gibbon's *Decline and Fall of the Roman Empire*, printed on patent ant-resistant paper. He tried to divert himself by recalling the themes of Beethoven's late quartets, but his brain filled instead with Bach's tinny Brandenburgs. He sat at his open door watching the steam rise from the jungle, day-dreaming about a suite in the Carlton Hotel in London, caviar and a beautiful companion. If God existed, and was kind, He would allow him to fulfil his life's allotted quota of delirial fever here, in a single marathon of enveloping oblivion.

After nine weeks the rains stopped as abruptly as they had begun. He set up his prospector's portable furnace and fed Morgan's gold sovereigns into it a handful at a time. He diluted the molten gold with one-third lead and stone chippings. He poured the brew into three-ounce moulds and, when the ingots cooled, stacked them in his portmanteau.

Leaving his equipment behind, Worth made his way by dug-out and steam-launch back to Manaus. He went directly to the Assay Office. The first ingot had hardly been proved when word of a sensational gold find began spreading through town.

In his suite at the Tropicale — not the Carlton, caviar-less and its only 'champagne' Portuguese — he washed and shaved. He summoned the best tailor in Manaus to attend him. Late that evening, he walked into the Tropicale's bar dressed in a white silk suit and two-tone shoes. Most of the customers fell silent and stared; a few continued talking. He banged a brass ashtray on the counter and loudly ordered drinks for the whole house.

A chair was hurriedly found for him to join the largest poker school in the room. The standard of play was abysmal; he had little difficulty in diminishing his new fortune by a minimum of a thousand *escudos* a round without his own losing strategy arousing suspicion. A man across the table claimed remembrance of an earlier friendship with Worth, when he had helped him out of an unspecified little difficulty — in Bogota perhaps, or maybe Georgetown. Worth lent him twenty thousand, which would never be returned, and went contentedly to bed.

Next morning, among the gathering of bank managers, concession-brokers, salesmen and whores trying to gain entry to his suite there were reporters from *Noticias* and *La Prensa* as he had hoped. By lunchtime, news of 'Cunningham's Gold Mine' was already on its way to the coast, by means of the newly installed Marconi telegraph.

Following by the express paddle-steamer, Worth dined at the captain's table in a cream mohair tuxedo he had selected for its surpassing vulgarity. His conservatively attired neighbour, a flush-faced, nervous man, said, 'Smithson. British Vice-Consul in Belem. An honour to meet you.'

Worth nodded pleasantly, and served himself to roast beef.

29

'Will you be taking up residence in our city, sir?'

Worth slowly chewed some meat and swallowed. 'I regret not. Now my labours are over for the time being, I am going directly to Rio to seek a bride, and then to Europe.'

'A misfortune, sir, for our own community's many unattached young English ladies.'

'Sadly, sir, it will have to remain so. Their mothers would hardly find me eligible. I am Nicaraguan-born, and without title or family.'

The Vice-Consul ate the remainder of his meal in silence. After supper, he approached Worth in the saloon, and sat beside him without invitation. He spoke in a low voice. 'The English mothers of Belem aren't so snobby as you've been told. They do it on a points system.'

Worth's curiosity was now aroused.

'Strictly confidentially, because I've taken a liking to you, it's perfectly simple. At the top of the scale, a native-born Englishman who's been to public school, even if it's not Rugby or Eton, can rate up to ten. If you're Scottish, you lose one point; if you're Irish two and if you're Welsh four. If you've got a university degree or show other signs of intellectual tendency, that's another two points lost. If you're in the consular service, they knock off three.'

'So under the system, you yourself score at most only fifty per cent?'

'It's not so bad as it sounds, old boy. Five is the top score for a locally-born Englishman, which is five more than a Portuguese chap can hope for. Unless the English family involved is in the direst circumstances and can pretend to find some hint of English ancestry in his lineage. In which case he scores one. And if he converts to Church of England, he stands a fighting chance of being elected to the British Club.'

'I suspect I have more than a hint of Portuguese blood in my own background.'

'Don't we all?' replied Smithson. 'I tell you where you fit in, old chap. The mothers are quite realistic. Belem is a long way from home, so they know they can't hold out too much in the way of titles and inherited money. So they score wealth on a

30

scale that puts it, at its different levels, only one point behind what they reckon to be the equivalent rank in the English peerage. I'll bet you're a Seven, if not an Eight — possibly even a Nine.'

'Why do you confide this to me? Aren't you concerned you might be exposing the young ladies to moral danger?'

'Sir, the moment I set eyes on you, I could see you weren't a Jayknow but one of us.'

'Excuse me?'

Smithson seemed momentarily puzzled by his ignorance. 'Just After You Know What. A chap who tries to touch-up another chap's sister.'

He paused, possibly having second thoughts. Then he shook his head sadly. 'So many fine girls. So few eligible men.'

'That's only to be expected, given the system you've described.'

'I think you'll agree, sir, that love is not a reliable guide in these matters. But please, not a word about my indiscretion to anyone. If you will permit yourself even a short stay. . . .' The Vice-Consul's face twitched, and he quickly stood up. 'I hope my frankness hasn't shocked you, old boy. Only trying to be friendly to a fellow passenger in the voyage of life.'

Before Worth could reply, Smithson had walked most of the way to the saloon's door.

Worth had hardly settled in a furnished apartment on the Praça da Republica when the Portuguese manservant Smithson had hired for him was bringing him on a silver tray, the visiting cards dropped off by the English community's hostesses in relays. The morning after their first conversation, Worth had established to his surprise that the Vice-Consul had no daughters of his own and had been disquieted by the apparent altruism. Clearly, however, the diverting of such a catch from Rio brought a reward of enhanced prestige, of which Smithson was surely in constant need.

Worth went from tea-dance to supper-party to the opera; to champagne (in reality, the mud-flavoured Portuguese imitation of it) on the lawn, to costume ball, to bridge at the club.

Each night, he kept in the privacy of his room a tally in a notebook. After a week he reckoned there to be around twenty plausible entrants to the Belem bridal race, give or take two, perhaps three doubtfuls.

He had few remaining doubts as to his own eligibility, by local standards. The girls' fathers and brothers were themselves at best four-pointers. They imitated the mannerisms taught in English public schools ineptly, having learnt them in local institutions. Judging from their conversations at the bar of the British Club, their non-commercial interests seemed largely confined to spear-sticking wild pigs and 'jayknowing' Indian girls. Their skills in literacy were reserved for reading bills of lading, the rubber market reports telegraphed daily from London and New Orleans and sea-mailed issues of *Sporting Life* and *La Vie Parisienne*.

Worth had not had enough advance notice to rehearse himself adequately for Belem. But despite his comparative lack of Anglo-Saxon bearing, it was unlikely that the mothers would launch independent inquiries into his origins and circumstances. Adverse evidence might be turned up, which could otherwise be allowed to rest unnoticed.

At their worst, the women — even the mothers — seemed preferable to the men. Still less educated, most were more pleasantly mannered and avid to listen to those echoes of European culture which reached their exile. They drowned the mosquitoes' whine and the cicadas' rattling, playing Chopin and Liszt on their pianos. Perspiring through their cologne water on to their petit-point embroideries of old master paintings, they read aloud to each other from the works of Miss Austen and Mr Trollope. On Sundays after church, the English community went to their pavilions on the coast. The men sat inside, drinking pegs of whisky. Women sat outside, sketching the seashore and laughing a lot when they thought they were not overheard.

Smithson had warned him that it was forbidden to interview any of the contestants privately before making one's choice on pain of being charged with thoughts of 'jayknow'. If you broke this rule you either went with the girl to the altar and joined her father's business, or were black-balled from the entire game, as well as from the British Club. On his side, Worth effected not to understand the approaches made by fathers for an hour of his time alone.

The rules were at least more straightforward than in Boston or London. Observing the field from the male enclosures, Worth pared down the list in his notebook.

After six weeks, he was left with one candidate: Angelica Hugh-Thompson. Her father was dead, and there was no business he would be obliged to manage. Her mother had sold it for an annuity. Angelica spoke excellent English, but with a Portuguese difficulty in enunciating 'h', 'k' and 's' — faults which, back in Europe, would lend usefully to their joint authenticity as colonists on a first visit home. Her eyes, her glistening bronze skin and her sleek black hair added the suggestion of Indian blood. As appealing to Worth were her courteous manners and her ready smile; those of a girl without inheritance, ready to repay a modicum of kindness and generosity with obedience and loyalty.

He addressed his letter of proposal to Angelica's mother. He was invited to lunch and prepared himself for interrogation.

In the dark-panelled dining room, a single clockwork ceiling fan turned too slowly to disturb the black flies which had entered through the holes in the window-nets. The table had been laid with the family's best silver. He deduced this not from its quality, but from Mrs Hugh-Thompson's inept attempts to conceal with her bouffant sleeves that the soup-spoon and dessert-fork in her own place-setting did not match the rest. Beneath the stiff-starched napkins were menus written in copper-plate, the purple ink blurred by the damp heat. Lentil soup, fish in white sauce, roast mutton with potatoes and Brazil cabbage, cabinet pudding, prunes and bacon on toast. The butler who served seemed unfamiliar with the house.

From the far end of the table, Mrs Hugh-Thompson stared nervously. 'Would you do the wine? I hope it's all right. Hughie — H.T. — knew about these things. Now I have to trust the Portuguese grocer when we have gentlemen guests to meals. Which isn't often nowadays. H.T. was in the nut trade.

Not as grand as rubber, but he was very well-respected out here. We used to have the Church of England Boys' Brigade annual jumble sale in our garden when he was alive.'

Angelica was sitting to his right. She was dissecting a fillet of boiled fish with her knife and fork, as though searching for a bone on which to choke herself.

The wedding was in St George's. They were married by special licence, because of Worth's pressing need to depart for Europe on business, and the infrequency of the steamship timetables. Smithson gave the bride away. The dean, a widower, said in his sermon that marriage was an institution indissoluble by any power but God, who had created it as a test of human endurance. Angelica listened to her embarkation orders with apparently solemn attention.

The reception was at the British Club. Smithson grasped Worth by the elbow and guided him out to the terrace. 'You've done our community a great favour today, old boy.' He spoke the bland words with a guilt-edged voice. 'I trust you've done yourself one too.'

They sailed that night for Hamburg, on the *Otto von Bismarck*. In their state room, Angelica co-operated in the consummation of their marriage with sensitive curiosity, if not with finesse. As she lay wrapped in his arms afterwards, he thought of Mr Smithson and put down the Vice-Consul's remark to an unfulfilled desire to 'jayknow' with a part-Indian girl himself.

3

The funeral cortege had paused by the flower-sellers' stalls in Upper Street, so that mourners could buy wreaths. Worth returned to the Rolls with a two-guinea confection of arum lilies. In its centre was a black-bordered card with the printed inscription: '*A BELOVED BROTHER, RETURNED TO THE BOSOM OF CHRIST.*'

Angelica said, 'He must have been very dear to you.'

Worth traced the outline of her ear with his little finger. 'They didn't have any *in memoriam* cards for half-brothers.'

'Were you close?'

'We never met. Our mother abandoned him when he was three; to run away with my father to Nicaragua. I found his name and address in a locked drawer in her escritoire after she died. It was in a sealed envelope with a postage stamp. So I wrote to him. He replied, asking for a loan of five hundred dollars.'

'He must have been a bad man.'

'It's little wonder in the circumstances. He said the money was to build a memorial for her. I understand he was very well liked.' Worth was displeased with the unpremeditated defensiveness of his tone.

'Then where are his friends today?' She bent her head away from his exploring finger, and was looking ahead at the one four-wheeler following the hearse.

He was weary of the effort of impromptu lying, to no great purpose. 'Presumably, they've been frightened away by the publicity. Have more respect.'

She lowered her veil. However necessary it had been to arrange it, he mourned the passing of Adam Worth. The

35

creation had resolved for several years the central mystery of his life: God's or nature's omission to provide him with an identity of his own. At least he was being buried in his chosen country.

His recognition of his fundamental anonymity had come to him not as a sudden revelation, but gradually — almost naturally. In early boyhood in Brookline, Massachusetts, he had grown up to answer to 'You'. Later, at the half-Lithuanian, half-Irish grade school, his classmates and teachers also addressed him as 'You'. He noted they addressed one another by name.

During playbreaks the rest of the children were unsure as to which of the two ethnic gangs he belonged and cared little. After school the mothers arrived. Each would go directly to her whelp or *kind*, grasp him by the hand and conduct him home. His mother, even when sober, stood at the gate and stared confusedly at the crowd of children, until he spotted her and went up to her.

Some days she failed to arrive. On his way home alone, he found that he could visit the same places again — the neighbourhood library, the cornerstore, the Russian Wild Animal Menagerie — and not receive a glance of recognition. Once, he bought a Hershey bar and realised outside the shop that he had left his schoolbag inside. He had had a hard job persuading the assistant that the bag was his, that he had been in the shop less than ten minutes before.

More and more, he absented himself from home for the impersonal surroundings of the library. He studied picture books about his native Europe, a place his parents mentioned only disparagingly. Through weekly immersions in *The Illustrated London News*, London became his favourite city. It was both grand and thrilling. Its fine streets and malls surely had no gin-breathed Irish policemen patrolling them, taking random side-swipes at passing children. It certainly contained no squabbling parents, but tall, kindly fathers in frock coats and lavender-scented, white-bloused mothers. In the private recesses of his mind, he naturalised himself an English boy. He secretly took the name 'Adam' from the street in which *The*

Illustrated London News was published, and 'Worth' from the brand-name of a make of touring bicycles which were regularly advertised in the magazine.

Soon after his estimated fourteenth birthday, he stole his father's pari-mutuel winnings from behind the picture of Betsy Ross stitching together the first Stars and Stripes. In Filene's basement bargain book section he bought *The London Almanac*, marked down because it was three years out of date. On his return home, his father confiscated it but did not beat him, or even shout at him.

His father said, 'I've a mind to pack you off to the Shakers. They can bring you up as a goy boy.'

'Papa, parents don't send their children to the Shakers. Children run away from their parents and join.'

'In my house, I'm the one who decides if a child runs away.' His father choked back an aggrieved sob and seemed to lose himself in contemplation. 'When you were a baby, you were so bright and good. Our village in Lithuania collected money together, so we could escape with you here, and you could learn to become a rabbi. Now you do this. It's not even a Jewish book. And stop pulling your nose.'

'Why aren't I studying to be a rabbi? Where's the money gone?'

'If you ever decide to become one, remember your father taught you the first lesson. Life is not just.' He threw *The London Almanac* on to the fire. It smouldered for a while, and put the fire out.

Worth had had a hardly less vague idea than his father as to who Shakers were, and looked them up in the library. They believed life on earth to be incurably miserable. The men and women lived separately from one another, and refused to have children of their own; they took in other people's and tried to persuade them to remain childless too. They waited impatiently for the joy of death, in closed communities in remote country-side. During the day they worked hard as farmers and carpenters. At night they prayed, drank blueberry wine and then danced frenetically, round and round in circles for an hour or more, singing, 'I am the Lord of the Dance, said He', until they exhausted themselves, and retired to their dormitories. The first Shakers had been English, led by a lady who had been expelled by the Quakers for saying she was Jesus Christ's sister. They had come to America from Lancashire, because there was more space to separate themselves from the rest of humanity.

He left the library dejectedly. On his way home, he took a discarded copy of *The Globe*'s evening edition from a litter bin at the tram stop. In it, he saw a reader's letter accusing the army of accepting boys under the legally minimal age of fifteen as recruits.

Next morning, he left home for school at the usual time. He went instead to the Massachusetts Infantry recruiting office in Cambridge. It was less than five miles from home, but he felt no need to escape further. His father would sit in the kitchen, tears provoked by ingratitude rolling down his cheeks, refusing to go as far as the next street to look for him, for fear of compromising his paternal dignity.

Faithful to the allegation in last night's *Globe*, the recruiting sergeant asked for no evidence to support his claim to be sixteen. He was given an enlistment bounty of one hundred dollars, clothing, a bed to sleep in and food to eat. What unkindness there was was different from that at home, and no greater.

It was in basic training that he began to perceive his anonymity to have positive potential. The disadvantage of remaining a number only to his superiors, Sergeant Balch and Corporal Carney— diminished prospects of their recommending him for promotion — was amply outweighed by his near-immunity to the punishments repeatedly suffered by his fellow squaddies, as the price of being recognisable. He could have less than pristine boots at morning parade three days in a month without being sentenced by Sergeant Balch to three days' fatigues. Consequently, he was able to sleep longer. As an experiment, he committed a succession of minor misdemeanours. Each time, Sergeant Balch or Corporal Carney treated him as a first-offender.

He decided on a bolder test and deserted. He bought a set of civilian clothes in the Faneuil market and checked into the YMCA. During the days, he wandered the streets of Boston. At times, he wished the military police would identify and arrest him and prove his hypothesis about himself wrong.

After a week, he went back to Cambridge and volunteered again, under a different name. The recruiting sergeant did not have him manacled and thrown into the guard-room. He witnessed his new signature, allocated him a new number and counted out a second bounty of ten ten-dollar bills.

The experience alarmed him more than he had anticipated. It also, during four near sleepless nights, excited him increasingly. He deserted again, and did not return.

For a long time, he found no work but casual labouring. Prospective employers with better, permanent jobs to offer were truly unimpressed by him. To provide himself with at least a veneer of identity, he turned to mimicry. He bought plain-glass spectacles and a small false moustache. He also rehearsed with a panama hat and a ten-cent cigar. He studied the speech and manners of a door-to-door salesman, and then was quickly taken on as a commission agent for pocket watches manufactured in Geneva, New Jersey.

He sold three to customers in Flanagan's before the bartender ordered him out, and to never set foot in the establishment again. He went to his room, removed his props, recomposed himself and was back in Flanagan's within two hours. He ordered a beer, which the same bartender served him. He began selling a pocket watch to the customer next to him. Ordering him out, the bartender said, 'And tell your friends. You're the second of you bastards we've had in here today.'

Awareness of his face's remarkable plasticity, and his control over it, developed rapidly. As he became more confident, he abandoned all but minimal props. Almost imperceptibly at first, his skill in mimicry began to be superseded by a sensation of being the individual he was impersonating. It was decreasingly a matter of imitation, and more as though he was composed of fresh potter's clay that he could mould to almost any shape he wished. Where within him his real self ended and his assumed one began, he could no longer measure with any precision. The relationship between them was ceasing to be that of ventriloquist and dummy. The illusion of the dummy taking on a life of its own was becoming a reality. Enough money and dedication and Adam Worth himself could be conjured into existence.

As he had told Morgan, the robbing of the Bayton bank had seemed the next practical step forward. As an assistant professor, he took to patronising the barber's shop next door, to studying its interior and wall construction while he waited for a vacant chair. At the bank he rented a safe deposit box, which he visited as frequently as was prudent. He went to New York by train and returned as a promoter of patent bitters from Brooklyn. With the money he had saved in the bank deposit he bought the lease of the barber's shop from its elderly owner. He filled its windows with bottles of bitters, for which there were few customers. One hot summer's weekend, he and three friends drilled and chiselled their way into the vault. He took for himself a sum he considered adequate for an English gentleman and left the remainder to the others. Worth sailed for England.

London did not disappoint him. Renting chambers in the Albany, he outfitted himself in Savile Row and the Burlington Arcade. He visited the Royal Academy, took tea at the Ritz, gambled at the Coconut Tree and dined at the Café Royal.

He did not affect to be English, surrounded as he was by the genuine product. But Boston was counted a respectable provenance — indeed the only such in the USA — and his good manners and ample means were evidence enough of the social solidity of the Boston Worths. He went to Royal Ascot and was invited to Wimbledon. He attended Henley Regatta and the polo championships at Hurlingham. He was elected to overseas membership of the Savage and Reform clubs, turning down the approach from the American Club. He dined in houses in Holland Park and Kensington, went to first nights and private views.

During working hours, he stole a few jewels, forged some letters of credit, cleaned out a pawnbroker in Jermyn Street,

40

and sold some share certificates in leading companies, which he had had printed to his private order. The facilities of London's criminal underworld were as refined as those of the other social milieux in which he moved.

Once he had married her, Margaret's attitude towards him deteriorated into surliness. He had responded by buying the house in Islington and leaving her there for long periods. Adam Worth's life had continued to be nearly idyllic, until a great fuss followed the disappearance of Gainsborough's portrait, soon after it had fetched the highest price for any painting auctioned at Sotheby's. He had returned to the USA with it while the trouble died down.

'Oh my Lord!' Angelica exclaimed. 'Couldn't you have let me stay on in Ostend until all this was over?'

He could hardly tell her that if he had done, there would have been little benefit to him in marrying her; but Angelica's distress was real.

The cortege had stopped again, on the steep incline up Highgate Hill. Two pall-bearers were pushing at the coffin, which had slipped backwards, snapping off one of the hearse's rear stanchions.

'We'll leave for the continent without delay,' he promised, 'after we've seen this through together.'

From Hamburg he had taken her directly to the Belgian coast. He had rented a suite in a hotel on the promenade in Ostend with an exceedingly dull sea view. She was uncomplaining and unquestioning when he took his leave of her to catch the steam-packet to England.

The aspect of London he had had to seek out was different from any he had known as a resident; and while he had need of its amenities, it had made him queasy.

To a greater degree than he had realised, the practitioners of each trade concentrated themselves in one section of the capital they could call their own. It was not just that physicians were to be found in Harley Street; tailors in Savile Row; cobblers in Chelsea; art dealers in Old Bond Street; and the lawyers, who litigated against them on behalf of clients who

41

found they had been duped, in Chancery Lane. The brewers were on the other side of the Thames, in Wandsworth; the quack herbalists in Hampstead; the fighting-bulldog breeders in Southwark; the female prostitutes in Mayfair to the south of Curzon Street; and the male ones to its north.

The undertakers were concentrated around Holborn. Walking the area, he passed the same establishments at least twice a day four days in succession, and rarely saw anyone bereaved entering, leaving or in the front offices, let alone any sight of a corpse. Evidently, most of their business was initiated after they had pulled down the shutters for the night. But where? One evening, he wandered into the Red Lion public house and found it crowded with undertakers, drinking gin with beer chasers. Two sat at a table in a corner. A man in his thirties, in a frayed suit with shiny elbows and drinkless, stood before them, negotiating. He gave them money and they left the pub with him. Worth had stumbled upon the funerary trade's clearing house.

He sat himself at a table on which four undertakers were playing dominoes. 'I'm looking for my brother.'

'If none of us is him, go and look somewhere else.' The speaker was a large, elderly Scotsman with red eyes and a pallid face covered in grey stubble.

'He came here to find work. He wrote home from lodgings in Lamb's Conduit Street. Then he disappeared without trace. My family's worried. He had weak lungs. He's in none of the hospitals.'

The Scotsman coughed on his Woodbine, and put down a one and a blank. 'Everyone's got problems. Why trouble us with yours?'

'If he suffered some misfortune and passed away, how can I establish the fact and waste no more time searching for him?'

The Scotsman yawned. 'If he snuffed it in a Lamb's Conduit lodging, you'll almost certainly never find out. He's either been dropped in the paupers' grave at Shoreditch or he's in the back of one of our shops, waiting his turn in the morning.'

'You bury people without knowing who they are?' For all his practical interest, Worth's skin was becoming taut and cold.

'They're not people,' the Scotsman replied. 'They're corpses. If a man can't be troubled to pin his name and address inside his jacket before he dies, what can we do about it?'

One of his companions, hardly taller than a dwarf, added a blank and a five at right angles. 'It's lucky for them they're buried at all, without leaving any funeral money in their pockets.'

A third said, more gently, 'We only take them because the lodging-house keepers pay us a couple of quid to get them out of their premises before the other tenants notice and give the house a bad name.' He laid down a five and a two. 'And almost half of that money goes on the coffin.'

Worth disliked gin, but went to the bar and bought a half-flask. He swallowed some down, and handed the rest round the table. 'Could I look in your shops, to see if he's there?'

'It'll be five shillings.'

Worth's hand moved towards his pocket too rapidly.

'For each of us.'

Before leaving the pub, the Scotsman collected his colleagues' keys. He escorted Worth from one undertaker's back room to the next, whistling through his teeth impatiently as Worth, striving to control his repulsion, peered through the dim light at bodies stacked on shelves and lying in uncovered cardboard boxes.

He completed the tour without finding one of the shape, size and features he required. He had concluded, however, that his guide was not opposed to irregular transactions. 'I'll meet you again in your shop at nine tomorrow evening.'

'It'll be a tenner.'

'A fiver.'

'It isn't your brother you're looking for,' the Scotsman answered. 'You're like one of those people who come and pretend to be doctors, wanting an unclaimed corpse for anatomical purposes. If it's to be none of my business why you want one, the price is a tenner to look and a tenner to take away the one you've chosen.'

The search took three evenings, at ten pounds a session, before Worth found a passable body. It was slightly too old and fat, with ravages of alcohol inscribed on the face. The proportions were near enough, and the rats would do the rest. For yet a further tenner, the Scotsman dressed it in a suit of Worth's own clothes, wrapped it in a shroud and placed it on a handcart he sold to Worth for two pounds, on condition he did not return it.

It was half-past ten. Pushing the handcart ahead of him, Worth set off along Holborn, towards Cambridge Circus. The sight would have been almost unthinkable anywhere further west in imperial London. Here it was almost commonplace after dark. He turned into Monmouth Street. A constable walking the opposite way, wished him a good evening without pausing.

He entered Sackville Mews, and unlocked the door of the workroom he had rented there. He pushed the handcart inside and changed his shoes for Wellington boots. He had selected the mews partly because it was unpopulated at night, and partly because it contained a sewer-access. With an iron rod bent at one end, he levered up the manhole cover. He fetched the corpse from the handcart, and dropped it down. He climbed down the metal rungs after it, pausing to pull the cover back into place over his head.

So proud were the Aldermen of the London County Council of their sewerage system, that they published and sold illustrated maps depicting white-tiled thoroughfares of effluent, named Fleet Street and Piccadilly, Strand and Pall Mall after the roads beneath which they ran. As well as studying the map with more than a rate-payer's curiosity, Worth had taken one of the sixpenny guided tours of the system, which the London Sewerage Board provided on Saturday afternoons as public entertainment.

Reaching the pavement of subterranean Shaftesbury Avenue, he grasped the front end of the shroud and began to pull it along. It was more relaxed after its fall. Above a torrent of dark, liquid waste that glistened in the light of his paraffin lamp and marked the crossroads with Charing Cross he turned right. Less than ten minutes later, after an easy journey, he reached the branch tunnel identified on the map as Channel Eighteen.

From his pocket he took a length of string — a precisely-measured forty yards. With his small hammer he nailed one end of it into the cement between the tiles. The air in the main sewers had been acceptably fresh from the speed of the current and the frequent airvents. The stench hit him as he entered the tranquil backwater. He lit a cigar and dragged the corpse up Channel Eighteen, until he felt the string running through his free hand reach its terminal knot.

He ripped the shroud down its stitching and pulled it off the corpse. Its face, beneath the blemishes, seemed a pleasant one, undeserving of the anonymous squalor of lodging house life in Lamb's Conduit. It was a pitiful irony that, so long as nothing now went wrong, he was about to receive after death a vicarious celebrity.

Worth felt his bones, which proved to have been sufficiently broken by the fall from the mews. He re-checked the contents of the pockets. A Sheffield stainless cut-throat razor, suitable for removing canvases from their frames. A map of the sewer system, with a route to Channel Eighteen marked on it in Indian ink. A plan of the National Gallery above, with a cross inked on to the spot where Ucello's *Battle of St Romano* hung. A letter to the Gallery's trustees, in handwriting identifiable to Scotland Yard's archivist as Adam Worth's, to be left in place of the painting, demanding a ransom of fifteen thousand English sovereigns, to be paid through the Pinkerton Detective Agency.

He turned the body face-down. Then he climbed the iron spikes to the manhole above. He pushed up the cover and looked through the gap with the aid of his lamp, into the National Gallery's lower basement storeroom. As he lowered it, he pushed the cover two inches askew, so that it did not fit flush with the floor again.

On his way back down into the backwater, he snapped off

the most rusted of the ladder spikes with his hammer. He dropped the hammer into the almost stagnant rivulet below, near the corpse, and then his lantern, which was extinguished and smashed. Taking hold of the string, he felt his way to the main sewer, and from there strode to Sackville Mews.

He stuffed the empty shroud into the workshop's stove. He added pieces of firewood and paraffin. He took off the clothes he was wearing and put them in too. He poured on more paraffin, set light to a box of matches, and dropped it in. While the evening's refuse burned, the late Adam Worth, naked, doused himself with buckets of cold water.

He also threw the Reform Club towel, with which he had dried himself, into the stove, which was burning well. From the cupboard he took his formal evening dress and put it on. He locked the door of the workshop behind him. The absentee landlord had demanded six months' rent in advance, so it would be at least that length of time before anyone opened it again. He sauntered up to New Oxford Street and hailed a hansom cab to take him to the Coconut Tree. He played *chemin de fer* until six in the morning, when he walked to Victoria Station. The morning boat train arrived from Dover, and he claimed Charles Cunningham's luggage from the depository. He went to the Carlton Hotel, where he had reserved a room by telegram from Ostend, and to bed.

He was sweating with fever. Standing above him, in a crumpled white habit, interrogating him about the previous evening, was the Pinkerton agent he had thrown off in Rio. Worth woke himself from his dream, and checked his temperature which was slightly below normal. It was after midday. He constructed in his mind the place to which he would retire after this final adventure was completed. The clapboard house of the New Hampshire farm was on a small hill. Pastureland, where cows grazed, sloped down from it to a lake, where perch jumped.

He breakfasted in his room next morning on York ham, pickles and China tea. As he did so, he read the penny newspapers. The space they had devoted to his departure from the world was more lavish than any he had been accorded while alive: two-thirds of the *Daily Graphic*'s front page, for example, its entire centre spread and a bold-type editorial.

The latter, he read first. 'It is with no pleasure, nor desire for gain in circulation, that this morning we devote fifteen columns to the inglorious end of Adam Worth. We do so because it is our public duty.

'It is a damning reflection of our time that a thief and a foreigner could gain more celebrity in the capital of the British Empire than many a dedicated engineer, surgeon, merchant adventurer or missionary. . . .'

The anonymous leader-writer's post-luncheon hypocrisy began to bore even its subject and he turned to the news.

The alarm had been raised by a storekeeper at the National Gallery. In the underground tunnel beneath, Inspector Jackson of Scotland Yard had found a rat-ravaged body. In its vicinity he had also found evidence which led the Inspector, later that morning, to accompany personally Mrs Worth, the American criminal's British wife, to Charing Cross mortuary. She had identified the body as that of her husband, without reservation.

Leaving the morgue, Inspector Jackson told reporters, 'I am going back to the Yard to close the file on Adam Worth, and to inform our colleagues in many other police headquarters around the world that they can do likewise. This is a triumphant day for detectives everywhere.'

Unless you were one of those employed on the case by Pinkerton. Supporting herself on the Inspector's elbow, the widow was silent.

Later, from an undisclosed hideout provided her by the *Daily Sketch* to protect her privacy, the widowed Mrs Worth told the newspaper in an exclusive interview, 'We were happily married. Whatever he's done wrong, he had good points. But I long feared it would end like this.'

Sitting in his Liberty silk dressing gown, Worth was displeased by Margaret's performance. Leaning herself on the policeman was passable enough; but a leisurely and inquiring reader, particularly after her reference to good points, could well ponder as to how even she identified the rat-ravaged

47

corpse with such quick assurance when the police could not.

It was, like the funeral she had arranged for him, cursory repayment for the letter he had sent her a week before, telling her that he was engaged on confidential business. He enclosed the key to his safe-box at Cox and King's in Pall Mall. If anything untoward happened to him, she would find in the box his life savings, a little over sixty thousand pounds, which she should not feel obliged to report to the Revenue for the levying of death duties.

His plan had involved the unknowing collaboration of perhaps a dozen people, from the storeman to Inspector Jackson. Of Margaret alone, he had felt a certainty. She would not have sat at home and waited upon news of the untoward before going to Cox and King's to check the truth of his letter. Once there, she would have helped herself to an advance. Other women in his past were more deserving; her greed had had to be rewarded, because it could be counted upon.

He called for a messenger boy and sent a telegram to Angelica in Belgium, summoning her to London on family business.

4

'*We brought nothing into this world, and it is certain we can carry nothing out . . .*'

Through the half-open door Worth heard the clergyman begin the joyless litany with which the Church of England despatched its members— or, in his case, a member's deceased husband— to the next world. He led Angelica into the cemetery chapel, wanting to be the last in to look over the congregation.

The chaplain on duty, a young man probably not long out of theological college, was standing on a small platform. He had his back to the crucifix and was facing the oak coffin. At least Margaret had not stinted on that, perhaps fearing that whoever was inside might have attempted an escape from a less robust model.

'Are you a relative of the deceased?' whispered the usher at the back of the chapel.

'Half,' he replied, loudly enough to cause some of those there to turn towards him. He glanced around the small, dim interior. Inspector Jackson was sitting in the rear-most pew. To his left was Sergeant Samuels of the CID. On his right, Worth at last recognised the occupant of the car which had followed Scotland Yard's behind the cortege: puffy-faced Thomas Snelling, the Pinkerton Detective Agency's Vice-President of operations in Europe.

'*Let us say together the Lord's Prayer, according to the words that Jesus Christ taught us. Our Father, who art in Heaven . . .*'

The usher, on tip-toe, advanced past five benches filled mostly with journalists, to a pew exactly half-way down the chapel.

'*Thy will be done, on earth as it is in Heaven* . . .'

Worth sat on the edge of the pew and leant forward, respectfully lowering his head into his cupped hands. Through the gaps between his fingers he saw ahead of him the arched, black-swathed back of Margaret and, kneeling beside her, a man he could not recognise from behind. The pedal-powered harmonium began to whine and the congregation rose from its knees to its feet.

'*Oh God, our Help in ages past, our Hope in years to come; our Shelter from the stormy blast, and our eternal Home. A thousand ages in thy sight are but an evening gone* . . .' At the front, the man at Margaret's side was awkwardly holding in his left hand a copy of *The Abridged Funerary Hymnal*. With the back of his right hand he was stroking Margaret's flank.

'*Time, like an ever-rolling stream, bears all its sons away. They fly forgotten as a dream dies at the opening day. Oh God* . . .'

The consoling hand had progressed to within a couple of inches of stroking her left buttock.

Most astonishing of all about the man's lewd caresses was that he was conducting them in the full view of perhaps thirty newspaper-men. Briefly constrained though they were, and as Margaret's companion was not, by the fact that a religious service was in mid-course, there were going to be unwelcome investigations before the day was over. The reporters as well as Worth might as well see who he was now rather than later.

'*Be Thou our Guard while troubles last* . . .'

Worth coughed sharply. The hand dropped to its owner's side. With schoolboy guilt, he slightly, involuntarily, turned, revealing a low forehead, a long, sharp nose and a treble chin. Immediately, the mystery as to why he had so casually disregarded the watching journalists was solved.

Worth recognised the man from the Coconut Tree where they had once sat opposite one another at the *vingt-et-un* table. Becoming bored by the man's abrupt and irrational play against the bank — if it had been him against Worth, it would at least have been profitable — he had gone over to the bar, and inquired of the steward who the man was.

'Lord Sebastian Howton, sir. He's not supposed to be allowed in here. They say he doesn't pay his losses.'

'Then why is he here?'

With each hand, the barman had dipped two used glasses into a sink of water. He had picked up a towel and begun to dry them one by one. 'I understand his uncle-by-marriage owns the *Daily Graphic* and the *Daily Despatch*. That's Lord Kemsley. His uncle's cousin, Lord Camrose, owns *The Morning Post*. They're both friends of Lord Northcliffe, who owns the *Daily Mail* and *The Times*. His brother's Lord Harmsworth, who owns the *Daily Mirror*. They give Lord Sebastian an allowance to gamble and whore, so long as he doesn't seek or accept employment in the newspaper business, sir.'

'Why doesn't the club send his bills to his uncle at the *Daily Graphic*?'

'Sir, it's called the Free Press. We have the gossip columnists coming in. They don't pay their subscriptions and they get free champagne. It's said that otherwise they'll write bad things about the establishment, get it closed down and put us all out of work.'

In the chapel, Worth turned his head briefly to the press benches, and saw the reporters concentrating on their prayer books. At least they would be able to return home to their families early that evening, instead of being obliged in the public interest to pursue the lovers late into the night.

'Let us pray for the peace of mind of the bereaved among us . . .'

Worth returned his eyes to the prayer book before him. It was the first Church of England funeral he had attended. To his resentment he saw that the chaplain had skipped his and the congregation's commendation to God's mercy of the departed soul.

'Our Almighty Lord, Who has chosen to take unto Thy judgement the soul of, umm, Adam Worth, grant we beseech Thee comfort and consolation for his widow . . .'

The Lord Sebastian Howton was granting it, at Worth's — or rather J.P. Morgan's — expense. From their discussion with Mrs Worth at the undisclosed address, the upper echelons of the *Daily Graphic* had found they had a woman with enough ready cash to at least have temporarily relieved them of the burden of Lord Sebastian, and to have tipped him off. It was enough to keep him in the style to which he aspired for maybe five years. While this lord was still more difficult to love than most, to Margaret the prospect of becoming a Lady through marriage, was comfort and consolation enough. So long as nothing went amiss for the three of them during the next half-hour, the private aspects of the arrangement would from then on be kept from prying eyes by Fleet Street itself.

'*Repeat after me.* [Margaret looked up at the chaplain.] *The Lord is my Shepherd. I shall not want. He maketh me to lie down in green pastures . . .*'

Worth could better survey his fellow-mourners in the open air, around the grave, just as Inspector Jackson and Thomas Snelling were enabled to look at him more leisurely. The presence of the police had precluded London's criminal community from sending even token representation, unless one counted old Jack Smith in his wheelchair — long since retired after losing a leg and half an arm in the unsuccessful Bristol bullion-train robbery. Alfonso and Mrs Hodkins, his valet and housekeeper in his Albany days, were in the small crowd. He recognised none of the others, some of whom appeared to be sightseers, who had selected a criminal celebrity's funeral in preference to Madame Tussaud's Waxworks, the murder trial at the Old Bailey or the Changing of the Guard at Buckingham Palace. The rest, perhaps half a dozen, must have been recruited for the occasion by Margaret and her escort from their less important acquaintances.

The reporters and photographers were keeping a more discreet distance than was their habit. By contrast, Sergeant Samuels and Thomas Snelling left the side of Inspector Jackson and took up positions close to the widow as the coffin was lowered on straps by the undertaker's men into the earth's cavity.

Worth joined the short line of mourners waiting their turn with the polished shovel. When his came, he bent down, picked up a clod of north London clay with his hand and crumpled it over the coffin's lid. Wiping his hand on his trousers, he walked up to Margaret and extended it to her. She did not raise hers to meet his and leant herself more heavily on Sebastian's elbow.

The sergeant and Snelling were studying the encounter closely.

'Mrs Worth, I am Charles Cunningham, your half-brother-in-law. It is so sad that we should meet for the first time on this occasion. I had just arrived in London to renew his acquaintance.'

There was no way of telling what was happening behind Margaret's three-layered veil, though he doubted tears. Sergeant Samuels had been bored by the exchange and was making his way back to Inspector Jackson. Thomas Snelling remained: the interest of the one was to shut the file, and of the other to prise it open again.

It was Sebastian who spoke. 'There's drinks at our house after this. Do come along. For a few minutes.'

'Your house?'

'Twenty-three Duncan Terrace.'

Worth's London residence, which he had bought to store Margaret, still had an inherent elegance; but the outward signs of it were faded. However she had been spending his remittances, it had not been on renovation and redecorating.

The front door was opened by a young Irish maid. There was no evidence of a housekeeper. Worth, his bride on his arm, stood in the hallway, waiting politely to be directed towards his own drawing-room, down the stairs from which floated sounds of unfunereal conviviality.

When they were announced, Margaret was standing in widowly pose, her back to the company, looking out of the window. The furnishings were much the same as Worth remembered them: a mock Adam fireplace, reproduction Chippendale chairs, Persian rugs that had been manufactured in Axminster. At first glance, only the fake Constable landscape which had hung above the fireplace was missing.

Worth took a glass of dry sherry from the tray. 'Nice home you have,' he remarked to Sebastian. 'Been here long?'

A heavy sea developed in the tumbler of whisky in his

lordship's hand. 'This is actually Mrs Worth's residence.'

'If you don't mind me saying so, you've made a fine catch in her.'

Sebastian's boyishly pink face, which within a decade was destined to have a vermilion flush to it, began to shine a little. 'I mind your innuendo very much.'

'No offence. After all, I'm speaking as a half-member of the family. Just a few words of welcome.'

Worth asked for directions to his own lavatory, which Sebastian gave him readily and with relief.

At the top of the second flight of stairs, he checked that Sebastian was listening from the landing below. Then he opened the door to the main bedroom. On the large brass bed were two piles of pillows, side by side. On the table to the left of the side on which Worth himself had sometimes lain was a half-empty bottle of brandy, the current issue of *The Pearl* — the English upper class privately circulated quarterly of pornography — and *Ruff's Guide to the Turf*. A pin-striped suit, which Worth recognised as one he had had made for himself by Hawkes, was draped untidily on a chair. Even judging by the standards of his own class, Sebastian was pragmatic, and fast.

When Worth came down the stairs again, Sebastian was back in the drawing-room, leaning against the mantelpiece and gripping his tumbler.

Worth went over and stood sideways to him, facing the light patch on the wallpaper where the fake Constable had hung. He put his mouth close to Sebastian's ear.

'Do you happen to know whether my half-brother left anything much? In the way of money?'

Sebastian turned and confronted him with the boldness of an aroused rabbit. 'How dare you ask that at a time like this? What damn business is it of yours?'

Worth placed a pacifying hand on his shoulder and spoke very quietly, 'It's just that a short while before he died, I lent him sixty thousand pounds, unsecured. I ventured to think — rather than trouble his widow — that I might ask you whether he made any provision in his will for its repayment.'

Despite himself, Sebastian successfully reduced his voice to a level still lower than Worth's. 'If you don't shut your mouth and keep it shut, and if you don't leave this house immediately and stay out, and don't leave this town and stay away from it until you've learnt some manners, I can have you thrown out of England before you know what's hit you.'

Worth believed him. He helped Angelica from her chair and into her black silk mantle. He bowed towards his widow, and escorted his bride down the stairs and out of the front door.

When he had de-coded Snelling's cable from London, William Pinkerton motored from Brooklyn to Madison Avenue to deliver its text to the old man by hand and without appointment. In the hallway, a footman telephoned for instructions, then escorted him to the West Room.

Morgan was wearing formal English day clothes, with the exception of a pair of bright blue canvas shoes. He stood behind the lectern, beneath the sixteenth century Swiss stained-glass window depicting the martyrdom of St Catherine. He was suffering from gout, in addition to his other ailments, and had found that the pressure he could apply to his feet by standing temporarily reduced the pain.

He read the message quickly. A million Morgan dollars had been as good as buried with Worth— wherever they were now, he could hardly instruct his lawyers to institute proceedings for recovery.

William Pinkerton stood in the centre of the room. He had taken off his hat and had positioned it in front of his genitals. His hands were nervously revolving the hat's brim, round and round and round.

Morgan's mind cleared. On this occasion, the wisdom of God had been greater than his. The Lord had disposed of Morgan's own choice of the Mona Lisa's thief, on account of Worth's unreliability and ineptitude, before any serious harm had been done, and with eighty per cent of the money allocated to the project still intact. Worth had been too greedy from the start. Morgan would now leave the choice of thief to the Almighty.

'Make up a list of all the best art thieves.'

'Being the detective agency we are, we have one already at the office, so that when a client's painting is stolen . . .'

'Remove all the copies. Bring them to me.'

'Sir, I cannot. It's in our printed library index, distributed to senior staff. If it went missing, I myself would have to launch a disciplinary inquiry. Furthermore . . .'

Pinkerton hesitated. Morgan's feet were aching. He leant his elbows on the lectern, on either side of Snelling's message, and stared.

'Sir, the list was composed for the purpose of apprehending art thieves, not recruiting them. It has five names. Mr Snelling has just witnessed the burial of the first. The other four are in jail.'

'Then get them out. And find some others. Start them on a race. Send Snelling to Paris to supervise. For the man who gets the painting first, two million dollars.'

'Sir, my agency does not . . .'

'When your men are out cracking strikers' skulls for Pullman in Chicago your agency doesn't seem to dither on account of moral quandaries. Mr Pinkerton, what was your agency's turn-over last year?'

'Over one and a half million dollars.'

'Of that, how much was contributed by Morgan enterprises, including strike-breaking?'

'Nearly one million.' Pinkerton involuntarily retreated half a pace.

'There's a half-million in this for you personally and up to another half-million in fees and expenses. That's a lot of money, Mr Pinkerton. And you'll have to earn it quickly. The Frogs and the Krauts are almost ready for another war. If the Mona Lisa is still in Paris when the German Army gets there, it'll be hanging in the Kaiser's bedroom in Berlin within the week.'

5

No matter how many times you have done it before, pensioning off a wife who has completed that role in your life for which you married her is rarely a light task. It poses difficulties inexplicable by logic, against which you have to prepare yourself thoughtfully. The first of them is this: while an undesirable like Margaret can almost be counted upon to accept hungrily the proffered consolation of money, the younger, more attractive, pleasant-natured and thus re-marriageable the woman, the less the prospect is that her response will be a peaceable one.

Until now Worth's mind had been largely concentrated on other matters; and he was suffering the further — to him, unprecedented — disadvantage, which made separation all the more imperative if the Mona Lisa were to be rescued from the Louvre. During almost two months of marriage the novel fascinations of Angelica's body and her increasingly bold caresses had marginally eroded; but, at the same time, his attraction towards her had grown inexpediently. Infatuation and crime were a dangerous mixture, especially in the territory of a thinking policeman.

By neither too much attention nor too little, he had carefully avoided giving her any hint of impending unpleasantness. He had opted to stage the final interview in a public place, where everyone else round them would be behaving with exemplary decorum. As he sat facing her in the first class dining salon of the London–Paris Royal Mail Express, he reminded himself that if Angelica refused his generous proposal, he possessed the ultimate threat: a one-way ticket back to Belem, her mother, and the irredeemable disgrace of having mangled the most advantageous match to come the way of the English community there in years.

On the table between them was a silver-plated bucket. In it, ice jingled in sympathy with the rhythm of the train against a just opened bottle of 1908 Bollinger. To his added unease, Angelica had managed, undetected, to remove one of her shoes beneath the table. In the privacy afforded by the enveloping damask tablecloth, her toes were fondly stroking the inside of his right thigh.

Worth sat himself as upright as was possible in the confinement of a South-Eastern and Chatham Railway Company armchair. Playfully but relentlessly, the toes continued their progress.

'Before you get too settled, I have decided to give you a grand tour of Europe.'

The toes paused, and then transmitted a small shudder. 'That's wonderful. I'd like to see Rome and Venice and Vienna and Carlsbad and Prague and Berlin and Dresden and, er, Copenhagen.'

'Whatever you want, my dearest.'

The pupils of her chocolate-brown eyes narrowed, as though a joke had misfired. 'Are you really that rich?'

'For you, Angelica,' Worth replied, deciding to bite the bullet. 'Spend a year. Travel on the *trains de luxe*. Stay in the palace hotels. Go to the best jewellers and dressmakers. Hire yourself a lady companion to share the pleasures with you.'

Her foot, at last, retreated to the floor. She was drinking consommé with an agitation Worth had not seen in her before. 'Why should I need a hired companion if I have you?'

He took a strong grip on his soup spoon. 'I shall join you whenever possible. But unfortunately, for some of the time, I shall be detained in Paris on business. Naturally, I shall write to you weekly and send you money as often as you need.'

'You've had what you wanted of me, and now you're trying to get rid of me.' It was not posed as a question. She spoke in a low voice, but overrode Worth's bid to reply. 'It's just the way the older women in Belem said men were. I thought before it was only true of their kind of men.'

He saw a logistic advantage in her misunderstanding; but he was pained by the charge. Two waiters in green and gold livery interrupted the conversation, while they removed the soup bowls, laid plates and cutlery and served sole mornay.

'If Paris is where you're going to be, it's where I want to be.'

'That is what I wish for myself too.' The ground was becoming firmer again. 'But I shall be fully preoccupied while I am there. And these days, Paris is too dangerous a city for a woman on her own. Every day, people are being attacked on the streets by armed robbers. Gangs of socialists roam around, stoning passers-by just because they look well-dressed enough to be the relative of a banker or a factory owner. If, like you, you don't speak the language perfectly, you may be mistaken for German, which is even worse. It's more violent than New York. Law-abiding men don't go out without revolvers in their pockets. The other day, the Prime Minister was injured in a shoot-out in the National Assembly.'

She was now attentively silent.

'So instead of enjoying the sights of Europe, you'd be a virtual prisoner in an apartment in a strange city where you've no friends.'

'Damn the sights of Europe.' She replied almost in a whisper. 'Don't you see I mean to help you?'

Worth ate some sole, while considering the impasse. As he did so, he saw through the periphery of his eye a pink silk handkerchief move into view and drop swiftly and accurately over the sterling fish knife below Angelica's right hand. The movement continued, as though without interruption, while the handkerchief and piece of cutlery inside it were transferred into her open handbag.

Worth was shocked. There had been nothing hesitant or clumsy about the manoeuvre; indeed, it had a fluency and grace which, in his experience, usually took several years to acquire. He recalled from their engagement lunch the substitute cutlery in her mother's place setting.

He recovered sufficiently to say, 'Why, you've no knife. What are railway servants coming to? Take mine, while I order another.'

She accepted the knife and placed it exactly where the other had rested less than half a minute before. With her left hand, she picked up the fork from her plate and resumed eating, as though passing from her mind a trivial lapse on the part of a waiter.

Only moments ago, Worth had been urging her to browse her way at leisure through Europe's better shops, carrying a passport identifying her as his wife with her. He kept a watch on her right hand. He wished there were means by which he could chain it to the table for the remainder of the meal.

'Would you be more comfortable,' he asked her, 'if you placed your bag on the floor?'

With a small smile — of wifely obedience? — she snapped it shut and put it under her chair.

Worth glanced hurriedly at his wrist-watch and remembered that it had been a surprise gift from Angelica during their stay in London. There were almost fifty minutes in which to reappraise his bride before the train was due to meet the cross-channel steamer on Dover pier.

While she, apparently contentedly, stared out of the window at grazing Kentish sheep, he studied the clothes she was wearing with new attention.

Although he found shopping irksome, even for himself, he had spent four days with her in the West End to ensure that the wardrobe she amassed for her European travels broadcast the tastes of Belem rather than Belgravia, of which he himself was supposedly as ignorant as she.

Looking at her, he could not recall buying her the cream, high-necked blouse made of wild silk nor the gold chain and filigree pendant, nor the straw boater with an azure ribbon.

'I am feeling a little unwell,' he said. 'Let us go back to our compartment.'

In addition to the handkerchief and the fish knife, Angelica's handbag yielded a solid silver pencil from Asprey's; a pair of crepe-de-Chine knickers with a Fortnum and Mason label; a string of black Bahreini pearls; and a Colt .32 smokeless, eight-shot lady's pocket revolver, with a stamp on its butt:

'Tested and passed by Army and Navy Stores, Westminster, London S.W.'

'Where do you keep your bullets?'

Angelica was seated in one of the compartment's two engine-facing armchairs, her lace-trimmed Empire skirt provocatively pulled up to within three or four inches of her knees. She pointed to a leather travelling bag on the rack. Worth bolted the door, took down the bag and began to transfer its contents on to the bench seat.

More crepe-de-Chine knickers, but from Liberty's in Regent Street. Three spun-silk camisoles from Bourne and Hollingsworth. A 22 carat cigar-cutter made by H. Simmons of the Burlington Arcade — presumably being held on reserve as another surprise gift. Seven pairs of brightly shaded cashmere stockings. An empty mother-of-pearl pillbox. Four bottles of Roger and Gallet's scents — he had bought her Yardley's more demure distillations. A manila envelope containing sixteen bullets and a large, damask-covered perpetual diary with a gold lock.

'How can I open this?'

Angelica undid the catch on the pendant around her neck and took from it and handed to him a miniature key.

16th: More dreary clothes bought for me by dear husband. Took nice scarf for self at Harrod's and very good? bracelet at Garrard's.

17th: Husb. with me all day. Only managed little ancient Egyptian scarab at Spink's. Dinner at Trocadero. Got so interested in husb. forgot to take any cutlery. But why has he these colonial prejudices about his wife's appearance?

He turned to the second page, which was blank. 'You stopped writing this diary over a week ago. Why?'

'I knew you'd find it.'

'Then why didn't you burn it?'

She took her time digesting the question, though surely not surprised by it. 'I know I'm not much good yet. I practised all I could in Belem, and you can see I've been trying my best since.'

'At what?' Worth tore out the first page from her diary, folded the sumptuous linen-rag paper in two and put it into the inside pocket of his jacket. 'The best I can do is to make a citizen's arrest, take you straight back to London, and have you charged and imprisoned for theft.'

Angelica pulled down her skirt ten inches or so. 'A wife can't be convicted on her husband's testimony in England. It's one of the reasons, they taught us at the Anglican Girls' School, why the English are more civilised than South Americans.'

The most ingenious thief in the western world was, for the moment, married not merely to a semi-professional klepto-maniac, but also to a bedroom lawyer. 'My evidence would have nothing to do with it. It would be that of your diary, the goods on this bench and the testimony of Aspreys', Fortnum and Mason, Garrard's and the rest.'

'You chose to marry me, not the other way round, and to bring me to Europe. And if you put me into Court, your name will be in the newspapers too.'

'You assume I'm not shocked by what you've done. You are more right in thinking I am worried about my reputation as your husband. You give me two choices. The first is to allow you to continue thieving as my wife, despite my discovery of your weakness, until you are caught by a shopkeeper who calls in the police. They will come and search whichever hotel suite or apartment you are occupying. The longer you remain unde-tected, the more stolen goods they will find, and the more you will blacken my standing as a good citizen.'

'The second?'

'If I'm not to turn you over now, is more Christian. When we reach France, we go to a notary. In his office, I hit you on the face twice with my hand— it doesn't have to hurt a lot. For ten francs, the notary writes out an affidavit that, in his presence, I have treated you with intolerable physical cruelty. We take it to a magistrate who dissolves the marriage for fifty francs. He orders that I assign to you sufficient French Government bonds for you to live comfortably from the interest. We go with the divorce certificate to the Brazilian or British consul— whichever you prefer— and a new passport is issued to you in your maiden name. Then you're free.'

There was a third possibility. They were drawing into

Ashford Station for scheduled mail pick-up. He could leave the compartment, as though to go to the lavatory, and get off the train, leaving behind Angelica and their luggage, legally and illegally acquired.

Angelica was fingering her pendant. 'How can you be "more Christian", if you're not one in the first place?'

'What do you mean?'

'The loose skin's been cut off the end of your thing.'

'How does a virgin learn about such matters in Belem?'

'They have bibles there.'

'The Old Testament is not a reliable guide to modern practices. Nowadays, many non-Jews have their male babies circumcised, for hygienic reasons.'

'Not in Belem.'

'How on earth do you know?' It was Worth who was flushed now, from trepidation about what his bride was going to disclose.

'During siesta time at the seaside on Sundays, when the grown-ups were asleep, we used to capture boys, take them behind the pavilion, pull down their shorts and have a look. You needn't be shocked. Wouldn't you have done, if you'd been us?'

'Is that all?'

She shook her head. 'Your name is not Charles Cunningham. You weren't born in Nicaragua. And you're not a gold miner.'

'Then who or what do you imagine I am?'

'You're a C.R.O.O.K. I don't like to use that word for you, but I don't know the polite one. And your name's Adam Worth.'

He settled himself on the bench seat, and remained silent.

'The last bit was the easiest. The night after I joined you in London you were running a slight fever and your mumbling woke me. After a while, I said to you, "Who are you?" You seemed to stay asleep. You answered, "Adam Worth." That explained what had puzzled me at the party after the funeral, so I went back to sleep myself.'

'And the rest?'

'I'd figured it out before I decided to obey my mother and

marry you. Nobody ever found so much high-grade gold in the Upper Amazon as you did. No man ever came out of the jungle after the three years you said you'd spent there in as good a physical shape as you. So either in Europe or the USA, you'd stolen that gold and smuggled it into the Amazon jungle. So you could bring it out again, and spend it as if it was legally your own. And as we've come to Europe, you stole it in the USA.'

'If you could figure that out at the distance I had to keep from you in Belem, there must have been others in the English community who did too. All the more reason for us to divide the proceeds and separate.'

'You don't know them. They're far too greedy to think. By the time you'd arrived to look over the prospective brides, half a dozen of the men had already gone up-river to look for your gold-lode. When they don't find it, they'll blame it on the injustice of fate.'

Worth was feeling much the same in his own predicament as she supposed they were in theirs. 'Didn't you think about the risks of becoming a real crook's partner? Have you seen inside a jail?'

'I've seen what it's like to have nothing to look forward to, but bearing brutish boy babies and wet little girls for a bullying rubber broker. Even if it goes badly wrong, I've no doubt which I want.'

A desirable and resourceful girl like you could easily have found for herself a less extreme ... No, it wouldn't work. 'Why and when did you start stealing?'

'Why, I don't know. Like most people, I started in the fourth form. We took pencils and chewing gum and things like that. We used to show off what we'd stolen to one another during morning prayers. I was much better at it than the others and, unlike them, I was never caught. I got frightened they'd tell on me. So I told them I'd repented. After that, I operated alone.'

Worth was winding down the window. 'How much money have you been making?'

'None. I thought it would be immoral. Just like in the fourth form we agreed it was wrong to steal from small shops, only

64

from bigger ones, with insurance policies. Except, after my father died, my mother went on about how poor we'd become, because the insurance company had refused to issue him a life policy, on account of his blood pressure. She wouldn't sell any of our family's valuables, saying they were heirlooms. When she was asleep one night, after she had too much port, I got up and robbed the house of most of its heirlooms. I put them in a box, pushed it and myself through a mosquito screen and threw the heirlooms into the Amazon. The insurance company paid.'

Worth put the revolver and the envelope of bullets on a pair of cami-knickers, from which he pulled a silk drawerstring.

'How charitable of you. What you didn't know is that insurance companies operate internationally. If you'd been caught stealing in London, or if you were caught stealing on the continent, information about Mrs Smith-Thompson's daughter would be fed into the international clearing house in the City of London. After several months' shuffling of papers, it would be matched up with your mother's claim. She'd have to give back all the money. You'd go on their wanted list, internationally, probably with a photograph provided by your mother. What do you propose I do with you?'

According to Worth's wrist-watch, they were eight minutes from Dover Pier.

He had wrapped her arms cache in the undergarment, and was tying it into a parcel with the drawerstring.

They were passing a field of hops. Picking up the parcel, he said to Angelica, 'Get ready to wind up the window again.'

He took quick aim and hurled it into the vegetation.

'Without my co-operation, you can't divorce me in France or anywhere else over here. You can't send me on the Grand Tour, even with a lady companion, for fear of what I'll do along the way. You can't pay me off with even half your gold, because what I want is to be with you. I don't know yet what you're planning to do, but I'm not so stupid that I couldn't help.'

Worth opted for the pompous. 'Blackmail is never a sound basis for a lasting marriage.'

'You were trying it on me a few moments ago.'

'To become unmarried. For both our sakes.'

'If you need to split with me now, even have me arrested, I'll never tell on you.'

At the age of forty-something, less than nine weeks into his fifth marriage, to his mingled alarm and curiosity Adam Worth found that for the first time in his life he was falling in love.

6

A Palace Hotel of the Great European Express Co. Central Heating. Elevators. English Bar. Private Electric Railway to Louvre. Director-General: P.J. Lebrun. Telephone: 85–23.
HOTEL PLAZA-ATHENEE
25 AVENUE MONTAIGNE
PARIS 8e.

July 2nd 1911
Dear Prefect,
   My editor has asked, Worth wrote, *for an article to be entitled 'Europe's Master Detective'.*

He glanced over the paragraph. He lifted the last two words from the page with No-Trace ink-extractor, and substituted: *Little-Known Master of Detection.*

I shall appreciate an interview with you at our earliest mutual convenience.

French officials had been ordered specially to indulge the American correspondents arriving in Paris to wait for the next European war to start. It was part of the new Prime Minister's 'Spirit of Yorktown' campaign, intended to prise President Taft from the shelf of neutrality to which he was trying to glue America's trousers. Prefect Lepine had more cause than most men of his senior rank to obey the directive, as the reputed lover of Hippolyte Caillaux, the Prime Minister's wife. But was the letter quite insolent enough to provoke a fast response? Worth changed the full stop to a comma and added: *over cocktails in my hotel.*
I am, Yours Truly,
Harold H. Bagnall

Chief European Correspondent,
Headline News Service of North America, Inc.

Acquiring an American news agency, so long as you didn't aim your sights high, had proved simpler, quicker and hardly more expensive than getting married. In New York, on East Forty-Fourth Street, there was a mass of third- and fourth-rate operations serving out-of-town papers whose credit ratings had dissatisfied AP, UP and INS. They mailed copy to clients on spec, billed them every third week and, when cheques didn't come in by the end of the following month, went under.

Before leaving London, Worth had studied the small ads in *Editor and Publisher* in Westminster Library, chosen the name and address of a broker, received from him by pre-paid reply-cable the list of availables, and bought — through a nominee company he'd set up in England some years before— *Headline News*, for its outstanding wage bill. He had telegraphed the editor money to cover salaries for three months ahead, and advised him to appoint Bagnall correspondent in Europe. This had been done next day.

Which was the more pleasurable sensation: the fleeting moment of supreme passion, or the peaceful mutuality which followed?

'I like your new face,' Angelica said, from her end of the bathtub, 'But why Harold Bagnall?'

'He's a journalist I met in Boston a while ago, with a pressing urge to part from his wife without leaving her a forwarding address. I bartered his passport for a spare British one I had.'

'But when his wife sees your articles appearing under his name from Paris, she'll come here and track you down.'

'She won't. She'll have her lawyer get an attachment-order on two-thirds of my salary. I've budgeted for it.'

'Doesn't it make you feel uncertain about yourself, changing your identity again?'

Worth leant the back of his head on the space between the hot and cold taps. 'It's said the alternative's to carry your personality defects around with you, wherever you go, like a portable prison. It's the great argument advanced against the benefits of foreign travel. And Lepine would hardly consent to meet with a Nicaraguan prospector on a honeymoon tour. Until I get a measure of him, we can't safely go ahead.'

He dipped the sponge into his glass, and dripped sherry between her breasts.

Beneath the Plaza-Athénée's glass entrance-canopy, an aide-de-camp held two Peugeot three-gear Super Vitesses upright by their handlebars, standing in front of them like a groom before a pair of thoroughbred hunters. Leaning against the wall was his own, more modest machine.

The Prefect of Paris [the reply to Worth had said] *does not think that his work as a detective could be recounted adequately in a single newspaper feuilleton. If you have questions to put to him, please be outside your hotel at 11.00 am prompt tomorrow, in attire suitable for exercise.*

Louis Lepine, almost as small and lithe as a jockey, was dressed in puttees, jodhpurs, a cellular cotton jacket and a reinforced white bowler hat. 'Put out your cigar,' he said. 'You may tell your readers the introduction of the bicycle to detective work is my most revolutionary innovation. It outpaces the most athletic criminal over any distance, and is conducive to meditation and good health during pursuit. Your FBI are denying themselves a potent weapon.'

'The FBI use automobiles.' It was a hot day. Worth wore plus fours and an open-necked shirt.

'The FBI also smoke cigarettes. Our previous Prime Minister had Renault build me an eight-cylinder cabriolet. If I rode round Paris in it, what would be the result?' He lifted and swung his right leg over the crossbar. 'Professional criminals would take to using cars too.'

He pushed off with his left foot, and started to pedal up Avenue Montaigne, towards Champs-Elysées.

Worth caught up with him after twenty yards. 'The FBI also don't use your *Psychology of Criminal Behaviour* as a textbook.'

A horse-drawn omnibus swung out in front of them, and both men had to brake slightly. Conducting an interview from the saddle of a bicycle allowed the reporter a choice between taking notes or steering and braking.

'The FBI's like Scotland Yard. Burying its head in forensic science. They peer through microscopes at dust, dissolve congealed blood in test tubes. They pore over fingerprints as though they were maps of Treasure Island. What they don't study is people.'

To their left was the Arc de Triomphe; to their right the broad, tree-lined sweep of the boulevard and, in the far distance, the dark silhouette of the Louvre.

Lepine went right, then half-turned his face towards Worth. 'They lack the sense of security about themselves to do what I do. Go out and hunt the criminal.'

Worth pedalled hard for two revolutions, and freewheeled. 'The objection's that your thinking's too influenced by Dr Freud of Vienna.'

'Freud and Lepine no longer speak to each other. He came to Paris and stayed in my house. He's a quack.'

'I have heard his drawing-room manners can be overbearing.'

'He brought with him a theory. A man becomes a thief because he suffers from the "English Syndrome". He has been born to an inattentive mother. This drives him, while still a baby, to transfer his mother-love to his father. The latter is jealous of him for stealing his wife, and rewards this attention with severity. The child comes to associate physical punishment with affection. When he grows up, if he is wealthy, he pays male prostitutes to beat him. If not, he steals, to have the state lock him up and chastise him.'

'Perhaps he was satirising your own approach.'

'Freud's humour was repressed in infancy. He could have been born in Edinburgh or Boston. If he's told a joke, he asks for it to be explained to him, and writes down the explanation. I asked him to our interrogation cells, to choose a suitable case for analysis, and prove his point. He replied that by definition, no one in there would co-operate for fear of being denied punishment. He took a train back to Vienna before breakfast.'

'If some of your prisoners are intelligent enough to be suitable for psychoanalysis, why did they allow you to catch them?'

'I concede it's irrational. The best of them could become rich by legal means. It's an unconscious yearning, not for punishment, not for personal recognition. That's why you always find a mental imprint at the scene of a crime.' His front wheel wobbled for a moment.

'Your FBI and Scotland Yard are transfixed by the myth that they're fighting a war on behalf of the rest of society against a minority class of law-breakers — what Darwin would call "a criminal species". Eradicate it, and you've eradicated crime from the world.'

Worth glanced at the cyclometer clipped to the handlebars of his machine. They were travelling at twelve kilometers an hour down the gentle slope towards Rond Point. Lepine continued, 'All non-psychopathic adults have criminal tendencies in varying degrees, just as much as they do the capacity to love, to sing, to reason. My own's very pronounced. When you break the law — I am not speaking of you personally, sir — I'll look into my own mind and find from in there why you've done it. That'll tell me who you are, and I'll then give you the recognition you crave without realising it, by catching you. Apart from his brain and his bicycle, the rest of a detective's equipment is toys and party tricks. Crime isn't a fungus or a germ to be probed in a laboratory. It's part of human nature, to be fought man-to-man.'

He back-pedalled, shifting the drive chain to the largest of the gear cogs.

Worth said, 'It was a modern scientific party trick that caught Dr Crippen.'

'A pathetic dentist. A profession not renowned for intellect. When he murdered his dreadful English wife — in my opinion quite understandably — what reasoning power he had was eradicated by panic. He caught a liner back to America, giving even Scotland Yard time to figure him out, while he confined himself on board.

'If only he'd taken the ferry to Calais, he'd have been in France before the alarm was raised. We'd have arrested him as a diplomatic courtesy, but not returned him to London to be tried and hanged. Our law is civilised. You cannot be extradited to face a more severe sentence than that for the offence in the French penal code, and his was a crime of passion. By now, he'd have been released from jail, reunited with his mistress, and no doubt be drilling teeth under an assumed name in Cannes. It's the menace of the professional international criminal that demands real thought from the modern detective.'

They were within a hundred yards of Rond Point. 'Think what modern technology's about to offer a thief. Count von Zeppelin has introduced his airships into scheduled passenger service within Germany. At the moment, they're mere tourist attractions providing aerial views of the Rhine. But the Count's Mark II designs are off the drawing board. Engines have been built, and have passed their bench tests. His agents in the US have acquired a tract of flat land in New Jersey. Soon Zeppelin airships will cross the Atlantic in a couple of days. A criminal will be in New York, celebrating that his theft was in Germany, the only police record of his fingerprints is in London and he's been absent from home so briefly the American police didn't notice he wasn't there. Celebrating that in the time the scientific detectives of three nations can assemble their forensic evidence into one piece, and sort out the wrangles between their conflicting legal systems, he'll be committing his next theft in Mexico City or Vladivostok.'

They reached Rond Point. The gendarmes had halted the traffic. Lepine's back straightened as he saluted them. He turned into Avenue Clement and accelerated. 'Put yourself into the mind of a man like Adam Worth. Look through his eyes at the opportunities already available to him.'

'I've just come from London. Scotland Yard were celebrating Worth's death.'

'Scotland Yard didn't know he was in England, until a sewer worker found his corpse for them.'

He steered his bicycle to within a few inches of Worth's. 'Do not publish this. I mourn Worth more than I'd mourn the death of Inspector Jackson or any FBI agent, let alone William Pinkerton. If only he'd come to Paris, he'd still be alive, in one of my cells. It would have been a rare interrogation. But his spirit will survive — unlike Dr Freud and Inspector Jackson, I'm a religious man. His soul will take up residence in another human being. Sooner or later, I'll find him, and publicly humiliate him. Otherwise, international crime'll become an epidemic.'

The driver of an open-top Samson, passing them in the centre lane, veered to the right to avoid a steam-lorry overtaking a horse cart coming from the opposite direction. Lepine steered his Super-Vitesse into Worth's, knocking the latter from its giroscopic accord with gravity. As Worth fell to the grass verge, Lepine and his machine followed them to the ground.

'Damn'd motor vehicles. But you're not injured. Remount.'

Worth felt the pressure through bruised ankles as they pedalled up to 12 kmph again. 'I propose a resolution to the conflict between yourself and the American police. *Headline News* will send you to the United States, as its guest this summer. You can solve some crimes committed in New York by European criminals who have outwitted the FBI.'

'Thank you, but criminal traffic is almost certainly to be in the opposite direction. The Americans have the money to pay for stolen goods, but little of value which is stealable in their own country. A European thief cannot put an iron foundry or a coal mine in his cabin-trunk. Almost all the great treasures are still on this side of the Atlantic.'

They turned on to the embankment, and began cycling alongside the River Seine. Worth added another three kmph to his speed, so as to turn himself on his saddle to address Lepine. 'Isn't it that your theory doesn't work? Dr Freud won't visit your interrogation cells. You won't accept *Headline News*'s invitation to America. Last night, here in Paris, were nine murders, excluding crimes of passion. Fourteen injuries caused by robberies with violence. Forty-three street assaults involving firearms. More than two hundred break-ins to domestic premises and one bank robbery. That's much worse than London or New York.'

'Those people aren't professionals. Times are harsh for

many French. The spring was late. Peasants doubled the price of food. If they were refused, they ploughed in their crops and left their animals unslaughtered. Factory workers demanded more wages so as to pay the grocery bills. Employers said they couldn't afford to pay because of the new war-preparations tax. The workers went on strike. The employers padlocked their premises and went to their seaside villas for as long as it took the Government to sort things out. The cabinet, because of the German crisis, has been too busy. Meanwhile, some of the workers have turned anarchist, some criminal, some both. What can I do? It's a problem for the politicians and the priests. Mine is to ensure that unlike New York and London, no major professional criminal can operate with impunity in Paris. To me, it's not a career; I don't even draw the salary to which I'm entitled. It's an obsession.'

'Why?'

'Two reasons. First, I was born to poor parents. After the last war, I won an army scholarship to law school. I used my qualification to make money, as a defence lawyer. I made a lot — more than enough to see me to the grave, and I am without heirs — obtaining acquittals for clients who should have been found guilty. I then decided I must atone.'

'Second?'

'In the war, I was an infantry sergeant. One night, my platoon abandoned me in the dugout just before we were to assault a German artillery post. I fired some rifles and threw grenades about to make it sound like I was a platoon. I charged, and a German sergeant, a corporal and five men surrendered to me. I became a national hero by default. France was short of them. Here in Paris, the President was pinning the medal on my chest and the photographers were taking pictures of me, and I became nauseous with fear. Seen in a civilian context, what I'd done was spectacularly criminal. I had a God-given talent to deceive and steal — to rob the Bank of France, if I wished. Why had God given it me? Later, I concluded that it was to enable me to understand and so outwit those who do wish to do such things.'

He paused. 'I shall transform my talent into a technique,

available to all detectives. But the jealousy is such, I'm dismissed abroad as a theoretician. A single article would not suffice.'

Worth said, 'I'll make it a series if you call me to you, when the next major professional crime occurs in Paris. Allow me to observe the method and manner with which you solve it. Publication will be on conviction.'

'A constructive proposal,' said Lepine. 'I shall consider it.'

They had almost completed the triangular route, and the southern end of Avenue Montaigne was in sight. Lepine reached out his right hand, levered Worth's left one from the handlebars, and grasped it. 'To collaboration.'

They turned the corner, Lepine looked towards the hotel entrance. 'What an extraordinarily beautiful woman.'

'My wife, sir.'

'My calling in life condemns me to celibacy.'

'I'd heard otherwise.'

'Press Club rumours. Compare my relationship with Mme Caillaux to that of a cardinal with his housekeeper. It has her husband's approval. Intimate but not physical. I cannot afford to allow my energy juices to flow anywhere but into my brain.'

Worth asked, 'What is your vice?'

'I am a nosey-parker. I am happy when I am prying into someone else's privacy. I've as many files about the behaviour of people who interest me, not all of them law-breakers, as Scotland Yard has fingerprint impressions.'

His bicycle glided towards the Plaza-Athénée. Dismounting and leading his machine by the handlebars, like a horse being walked to its stable, he went up to Angelica and gazed into her eyes. He took her hand in his, bowed and kissed it. 'You are welcome in Paris, but beware of petty theft, madame.'

He turned to Worth, and gave him a sheet of paper. 'If you wish to become sufficiently active, mentally, to keep up with me, cycle regularly and follow this diet.'

The writing was bold and neat, mimeographed in purple ink.

Breakfast: 2 raw eggs, beaten (no salt). 1 glass goat milk.

Lunch: 1 tomato. Steamed white fish. 2 apples. 1 glass red wine.

Dinner: Bouillon. Half-kilo grilled lamb, calf or foal brain. 1 lettuce. Half Camembert cheese. 3–4 glasses red wine.

Just before dawn next morning, Jacob and Cie, a large mill on the banks of the Canal St Martin in northern Paris, making tarpaulin for the French Army, burst into flames. A night-watchman was killed by the initial explosion. The smoke suffocated two firemen.

A special edition of the anarchist daily, *Demain*, announced it as a victory for the working class in their struggle against capitalist oppression and war. A few hours later, rightwing newspapers were demanding the arrest of *Demain*'s editor, for sedition. The liberal *L'Intransigeant* suggested that the only victors were Germany and anti-semitism. The anti-semitic clients of the *Relais des Patriots*, where Worth and Angelica breakfasted, held that the fire had been started by the Jacob family themselves, so as to emigrate to the USA with the insurance money. The US Ambassador, Mr Fergus, said in conversation with American reporters, 'The French aren't only hurling themselves into a pointless war against Germany, their natural allies. They're squabbling with one another all the way to the battlefield. It'll be a war in which our country and our British friends will take no part.'

As the crisis worsened, Paris seemed outwardly to conform ever more to its own platitudes. By ten o'clock, the morning mist had risen from the River Seine. The cloud of soot from the now smouldering mill had thinned to a filigree. It wafted on the eastward breeze above the centre of the city, glistening in the summer light like a translucent gold canopy.

In the open-air cafés beneath, it was already hard to find a vacant seat. Bed-wearied couples strolled arm in arm in the Place de l'Opéra, through the gauntlet of robed Algerians trying to sell Eiffel Tower inkstands, Nôtre Dame music boxes and tickets to unlicenced places of entertainment. A street salesman of pictures of Parisian scenes had set up an easel next to a flower seller's stall, and was pretending to work on a watercolour of the stepped side-alley leading up to Montmartre and the Sacré Coeur. In the alley, two coiffeured poodles, their leads dragging, smiled as they copulated.

Worth and Angelica turned the corner into the Rue de Rivoli. They walked rapidly past silk shops, perfumeries and jewellery showrooms. As they came nearer to their destination, these gave way to smaller, seedier shops, with signs in English. One had a window display of Sèvres porcelain pillboxes, soup tureens, dinner plates and ashtrays bearing replicas of the Mona Lisa. Next door was a photographer's studio, where you could have your portrait taken, peering through the gap which had been cut out of a reproduction of the Mona Lisa, replacing her face with yours.

They stepped around an elderly man in a crumpled raincoat, on all fours, copying in coloured chalk on a paving stone a twenty-centime print of Mona Lisa. As they did so, they crossed a boundary of light, from sunshine into grey shadow.

Angelica's hand lightly gripped his elbow. They looked across the street, up at the grimy, looming north wall of the Louvre.

'It's like a jail,' she said.

'That's because it is one.'

For Worth as well, it was the first glimpse of the building from which they were to spring its most famous prisoner. In libraries in New York and London, he had studied the Louvre's architectural history, design and structure, so intently and in such detail that he had come to feel almost at home in the museum before setting foot in it. For all his preparations, he had not braced himself for its cold, forbidding spirit.

Yet it was through no oversight nor irony that the French held the Mona Lisa captive in a building which had first been constructed as a moated prison for the incarceration of foreigners. The French, like the English and the Americans, had had little talent of their own for creating great art. As the English had also done, and the Americans were now doing, they had bought, smuggled, stolen and looted it from southern Europe, the Ottoman Empire and the Orient. A work of art was not a source of joy or sadness, contemplative pleasure or sudden excitement, but plunder. The moral justification, when one was called for, was that the French were the safe-keepers of the world's cultural inheritance, guarding it for future generations against the kind of carelessness which had allowed it to fall into their hands in the first place.

'Who is this woman of extraordinary beauty, smiling so enigmatically at us? Chewing gum in her presence is forbidden. Is she Giradino's daughter, born in 1479, who seventeen years later became the second wife of Francesco del Gioconda, a money-lender?

'Or is the haunting image known to us as Mona Lisa — Mistress Lisa — the genius Leonardo da Vinci's vision of the divine essence of femininity?'

The guide expelled hayfever phlegm from his throat into a green handkerchief. It was the second of eight times that day he was to give his four minute lecture in English, and already his voice was thinning.

Not that this mattered to the two hundred or so tourists who crowded the shabby, square room. They hadn't paid him thirty-five centimes each, in addition to the fifty centime admission charge, for his knowledge of art. The Louvre was not only the murkiest of the world's major museums. It was the largest, and was without signposts. The function of the guide was to pilot one rapidly through the maze of stairways, corridors, galleries and *salons*, crammed with ancient Egyptian bric-à-brac, Armenian ikons, Chinese ceramics and vast canvases depicting French military victories, to the Mona Lisa.

'Now we shall turn our attention to the celestial background, before which Lisa floats, one might say, like an angel. . .'

Angelica's hand in his, Worth turned out of the Salon Carré and into the Grand Gallery. His first glimpse of the security precautions was discouraging. One could see the route of the electrical alarm wires to the control box beneath the flocked purple wallpaper. The flooring in front of the painting had been carpeted, presumably to conceal electric pressure-cushions, which could be switched on during the hours the Louvre was closed to the public.

With his fingertips, Worth wiped dust from a pane in the window of the Grand Gallery, directly opposite the Salon Carré's main exit. The courtyard outside was vast — perhaps four hundred yards wide — flat and treeless. On two sides, to the north and west of the museum, it was overlooked by the well-cleaned windows of hundreds of government offices. The fourth side was open, giving a view to and from the Tuileries Gardens.

The Salon Carré had a doorway. It led into a long corridor, with windows facing south, over the broad riverside promenade, the Seine itself and the elegant blocks of apartments on the opposite banks. The only cover available was the moat. This had been filled with rubble, which had been covered with cobbles to within eighteen inches of the level of the adjoining pavement.

With such security on the outside, what need had the museum authorities to protect even their most valuable exhibit on the inside with more than a couple of alarm systems to deter vandals? A professional might continue to hide in the museum until after it closed for the day. Unless there was a third, better-concealed electric circuit — and why should there be? — he could rewire the first two and take the Mona Lisa from the wall, between guard patrols.

He then had three choices. He could break out of the building with her, and be seen doing so no matter which route he chose. He could return with her to his hiding place for the remainder of the night. However negligent the night guards (and in Worth's experience, few men took such a job unless they were) the day shift would come on duty at eight, and find the painting missing. The museum would remain closed for as long as it took to retrieve her and hunt down her kidnapper.

The third option was that he could rehang the Mona Lisa on the iron hooks from which he had lifted her, repair the alarm systems, and sneak out of the museum empty-handed with the first departing flock of tourists next morning.

Worth and Angelica went silently back to the Salon Carré.

'To technical matters. Now you see Mona Lisa is not the big painting most of you imagined. Size is not greatness. You have known her until this moment through enlarged reproductions. It is an offence under French law to make a copy which is not at least one third larger or smaller than the original.

'It is thirty-eight inches in height, and twenty-one inches wide, making a surface area of 798 square inches. King Francis I of France bought her from Leonardo for eleven thousand ounces of gold. This would put a value on it, if it were to be sold today, of more than thirteen ounces of gold per square inch. There is no recorded sale of any painting before or since, no matter how masterly, which has fetched as much as one square inch of Mona Lisa would.

'It is also the heaviest masterpiece, for its size, in existence. The sensation it conveys, of celestial lightness, is an illusion. Mona Lisa is painted not on canvas, but on a block of Tuscan poplar, over two and a half inches thick. Together with its frame and its protective glass, it weighs 182 pounds. To lift it from the wall requires special training and two strong men.'

The guide departed rapidly to fetch the next group from the lobby, and most of the tourists left the musty, muggy room almost as quickly. Worth and Angelica remained with the stragglers trying to perceive, in the few moments left to them before another two hundred were marshalled into the room, what it was that was great about the Mona Lisa.

If the faded original was as powerful as the tinted reproductions of her, drawing-pinned to schoolroom walls, or at least one's memories of them, the Louvre's curators concealed it with thick glass and poor lighting. You could see little more than a woman with an oxide complexion and a nose slightly too large for her face, seated before a wobbling landscape. The naturally firm line of her breasts had been flattened with black paint, applied perhaps at her husband's, perhaps at her father-confessor's insistence, implausibly representing a high bodice.

How would J.P. Morgan react, inspecting it privately in whichever of his dark retreats he intended to die?

As the financial saviour of the French Government, after its own central bank failed, he was the only living foreigner for whom the curators had been ordered to take Mona Lisa from behind her distorting window, to be displayed to him for a few minutes in sunlight, despite the minor fading incurred.

Worth peered again through the protective glass. From the south corridor came the approaching sound of tramping tourist feet. He glanced around the room. There were seven people left.

One man sat by himself on the wooden bench in the centre. He was in his mid-forties, about thirty pounds overweight and almost bald. His face had a midday sheen.

He held a small, leather-bound pad in which he was making notes with a propelling pencil, the silverplating of which had worn through in parts to the brass.

Worth said to Angelica, 'I'll see you at the hotel.'

7

Worth had thought little about Thomas Snelling since the funeral in London.

'I didn't know Pinkerton employees to be connoisseurs of the fine arts.'

Snelling started defensively. 'Even on business, a man can't visit Paris without paying a call on Mona Lisa.'

He rose from the bench, replacing his note book and pencil in his waistcoat pocket. A detective's self-respect was impaired by being recognised by someone he did not. To admit to a person as well-dressed and -spoken as Worth, even temporary failure of recollection could lose your firm a potential or actual client.

'I myself have had enough art for today. I'd welcome American company. Join me for lunch.'

Snelling's unease increased. 'In this town, I pass up lunch.'

'You have an aversion to snails, frogs' legs, cow's stomach and lambs' brain?'

'Not at all, sir. I come from Cincinnati. I don't know how long you've been in Paris, but the French smother their food with sauces, so you can't judge how stale it is. The sauces aren't good, so the natives swallow down their meals with wine. And if you think the wine they ship across the Atlantic is poor, you should steer away from that they drink themselves.'

Worth said, 'My suggestion is the Brasserie San Francisco. The specialities are oysters, steaks and potatoes and Pilzen beer.'

In the taxi, Worth said, 'You seem a sporting gentleman, sir. Are you hungry?'

'What's behind your question?'

'If you've not visited the San Francisco before, I should warn you it's something of a club. The rule is either separate checks, or you register a table bet with the waiter before you eat.'

'I'm fairly new to this town, sir. What's a table bet?'

'This year's fashion. You aim to eat your way through the menu. The diner who gives up first, pays. If you both get to the end, the meal's on the house.'

'Does the menu have any cow's stomach?'

'No sauces either. Strictly oysters, four varieties, opened from the barrel to order, six to a plate. Four cuts of ten ounce steaks. Potatoes: French fried, sautéed with onion, braised in cream or tossed in mayonnaise. Salad: lettuce, endive, chicory, tomato. Four cheeses: two hard, two soft. Beer or Bourbon. Coffee with Cognac brandy.'

'I haven't had a square meal since I left London,' said Snelling.

Snelling drenched half a dozen *Bellons de luxe* with pepper sauce and tipped them one after another from their half-shells into his mouth. He gulped some beer, and reached for the bread basket.

'Leave the bread. We've a long way to go.' The second of Worth's oysters was still poised on his fork. The advice was not altruistic.

They were brought two grilled entrecôtes with matchstick potatoes.

'That's for another table, my friend,' Snelling said. 'We've three more plates of oysters to come.'

The waiter looked towards Worth, who motioned him to serve the steak. 'There'll be more oysters later. After we finish the first sequence of steak, salad, cheese, coffee and brandy.'

'Don't think I'm doubting you, sir, but before we continue, I'd just like that confirmed by the manager.'

'The rules are printed on the back of the menu.'

'I don't read French.'

'Unfortunately, the manager speaks no English. Whether because he can't or won't, only he knows. If you suspect I'm trying to take advantage of you in any way, the bet's cancelled.'

Worth cut into his steak, causing blood to ooze from it on to the plate. 'Meanwhile, eat and drink as much as you can manage as my guest.'

After a few moments' hesitation, the meat before him cooling untouched, Snelling capitulated to cowardice. 'I'm no quitter. A bet's a bet.'

A man on a Pinkerton salary and expenses couldn't afford to lose. If Snelling didn't have that notebook in his pocket, Worth would have found a way to let him win.

Snelling's spirits rose as he came to the third hurdle of his second canter down the menu. He was leading by five dishes. While Worth hesitated over his Gruyère, with a *demi-tasse* and Cognac next, Snelling had raced ahead through six first-grade *Claires* and *filet mignon* with sautéed potatoes and onions. He forked the contents of a small bowl of chopped endives into his mouth.

'Where did you say we'd met before?' Snelling asked.

'If you don't recall, sir, I trust there's no mistaken identity. I thought you to be a mutual acquaintance of that fine Englishman, Inspector Jackson. What brings you to Paris?'

Snelling drank Pilzen. 'I hope Larreen's one of those flies on the wall, watching me now.'

Worth glanced around the bare white walls. The Brasserie San Francisco was too successful a restaurant to have to barter luncheons for sketches with those young, upstart artists, Braque, Léger and Picasso. 'There are no flies, Mr Snelling.'

'Larreen's my wife. We first got together at high school, at the Community Chest spaghetti-eating contest on Labour Day. The teachers tied our hands behind our backs, and you had to bend your face over the bowl and suck the spaghetti up into your mouth. I shan't demonstrate in this elegant restaurant. She came first: I was second. This beer is acid. Have the waiter bring Bourbon straight up.'

Even by the standards of the Pinkerton Agency, Snelling was resilient. Over the next forty minutes, he emptied three glasses of whisky, while advancing his lead over Worth to over a full lap of the menu. There was one more to go.

'I hope you're enjoying this. Ask the waiter to bring my hors-d'oeuvre with my coffee and brandy. You know what they say at home about people like you? God put your stomach in your eyes.'

Snelling's paling came suddenly. Oysters harvested from the rocks off St Malo in Brittany were by far the largest found on the European coasts. Uniquely dense in consistency, they were yellowish with blue veins. The aroma, which further enhanced their market price, was of the khaki, bulbous seaweed Bretons also savoured.

Snelling put two in his mouth and attempted to swallow them. He chewed, and tried again.

Worth turned his eyes to his *contre-filet*, with steamed potatoes in sour cream.

Snelling began to make a very quiet choking sound.

Worth raised his eyes enough to pick up and hand him his glass of whisky.

Snelling was breathing as rapidly and deeply as a Chicago commodity trader. His face was as bleached as a skeleton's. His right hand let the glass slip and moved with his left down to the sides of his chair.

Worth said: 'The men's room's straight ahead.'

He gave Snelling four minutes. As Worth passed the bar, on his way to investigate, he collected a bottle of Fernet-Branca.

Snelling hadn't had time to bolt the door. Worth found him, his trousers and Fruit of the Looms pushed down to his calves, supporting himself against the cubicle's corner-joists.

'What the hell kind of toilet is this with no seat?' he demanded.

'Have your feet feel their way back to the footsteps. Don't hurry. Now keep them there. Put your hands on my shoulders. Let my shoulders take your weight. Bend your knees. Keep that right hand on my shoulder. Mr Snelling, you can't afford the luxury of holding your nose.'

'I think I'll be sick instead,' said Snelling.

Worth steered him to the washbasin, and helped him unbutton his jacket and waistcoat.

During his first long retch, Worth reached into his pocket and took his notebook.

Snelling's vomiting subsided and then ceased. He remained leaning over the basin, panting. Worth poured two inches of Fernet Branca into a glass.

'Drink it.'

The aroma alone was enough to make Snelling splutter.

'It tastes worse. Swallow it straight down.'

As the acrid liquor penetrated his system, his whole body complained with a shudder. 'I'm going to throw up again.'

'One doesn't. You won't.'

Snelling stopped shaking. His breathing calmed. He straightened himself. He turned on the faucet and splashed water on his face.

'Button your clothing back into place. I'll settle the check for you. Give me your billfold.'

'I don't know how to say this,' said Snelling, meaning that he did, but distrusted the consequences. 'I've only two francs fifty on me. I didn't count on losing.'

'I'll advance you. Repay me tomorrow.'

To Snelling, tomorrow seemed like a far-off paradise. 'Sir, what am I to do about this afternoon? I can hardly conduct business in this condition.'

'It's out of the question.' Before Snelling recovered, Worth needed more time with him, to obscure the tracks of the notebook which was now in his trouser pocket. 'The custom's for the winner to treat the loser at Madame Wilson's.'

Claudette Wilson had achieved her English surname by having been, briefly and long ago, wife to the British ambassador's butler. In the divorce proceedings, Mr Wilson's lawyer asserted that she had little personal inclination for intimacies with the opposite sex, and had married to gain entrée to the diplomatic corps for commercial reasons.

Her business had grown during the years since to occupy five floors of a purpose-built mansion in Rue Washington, between Champs-Elysées and Boulevard Haussmann. Contrary to Civil Decree 118 of 1906, governing the supervision of brothels, these premises were unlicensed. This was not, however, because Madame Wilson was either disreputable or covert.

Decree 118 not only empowered but obliged the *polices*

sanitaires to make regular inspections of licenced establishments, during business hours. To enter unlicenced premises uninvited — and such invitations were by definition not to be had — the agents needed to raise a search warrant, if they were not themselves to risk being charged with trespass.

Prefect Lepine ensured that no such warrants were issued in Madame Wilson's case. The distinguished men who patronised her establishment were encouraged to feel that, there, they could briefly escape the burdens of public life unobserved.

'You mean I can have any girl in this room and you'll pay?' Snelling sat next to Worth on a stool at the bar of the *salon d'invitation*, which Madame Wilson had had redesigned and decorated as a replica of the Neptune Lounge of the newly-launched luxurious ocean liner, the Titanic.

He was drinking dark Bordeaux rum laced with grenadine. Since leaving the restaurant, his recovery had been disconcertingly rapid. Worth had suggested he switch drinks.

'Make your choice.'

Snelling asked: 'Which one's your fancy?'

'It'd be inhospitable to tell you. She might be yours too, and you might feel obliged to defer to me as host.'

'That's what I intend, sir. I'll have her after you. That way, I'll know she's clean.'

'I'm not sure I understand you, Mr Snelling.'

'Call me Tom. Clearly, you're a regular. So you know which of them have VD.'

'The establishment's patronised by the American Embassy, the *New York Times* bureau and the Chase Manhattan Bank. American Express refer only their most discerning clients.'

Snelling turned on his stool and looked beyond the white marble fountain — a feature not to be found on the Titanic — that spouted a fine spray of crystal water through the upturned vulva of the Goddess Aphrodite. On the damask-covered sofas beneath the fake portholes, fourteen girls remained from the junior league of the afternoon shift. Their uniforms were made from ostrich feathers.

'You like coloured girls, Tom?'

'Yes, sir, but not in the way you imply. To use a negress to slake your lust is to insult their race. That's what the American civil war was about.'

'If you don't mind waiting, as she seems to be presently occupied, there's a sixteen-year-old Episcopalian from Boston. Madame Wilson took her in after she absconded from her family's cultural tour of Europe. The third from the right's a Swiss. She coats herself with chocolate sauce for you to lick off.'

'How about the end one on the left?'

'Fine, if you don't mind her having a penis as well as a vagina.'

Snelling's confusion grew. His breathing became more impatient. 'You choose for me.'

'Do you prefer larger breasts or smaller ones? Abundant pubic hair or none?'

'My mother's big-breasted.'

Snelling's quizzical eyes ranged the line again, and stopped. 'That's her,' he said.

He pointed a trembling index finger at a large, blonde Alsatian woman. Her pendulous breasts seemed to have been swollen and re-firmed by cellulose injections.

Snelling snorted, perhaps with pleasure, as he mounted the stairs behind her. In his current condition, whatever the quickening of libido inspired by separation from Larreen, he was going to be a half-hour.

While he waited, Worth did not dare take out and examine the notebook pressing against his left buttock. He glanced again at the slender, ebony African seated next to a far larger one, at her bright eyes, her indecipherable smile, her near-perfect limbs. Angelica's frequent affections gave him sparse surplus appetite, or justification for infidelity. Equally, he had no inclination for more alcohol, and had in past idle moments speculated without resolution on a private anatomical mystery concerning the black races.

'Before you become too interested,' said the grey-haired, black-frocked lady behind the bar, who kept the accounts, 'they're two hundred francs the hour.'

That was four times the evening rate for a first-team girl.

'I've twenty-five minutes. I'll just take the small one. Bill me for fifty.'

The old woman looked in her book. 'Clara will be down in time. She's also black, and I can have her give you an excellent fellatio.'

'What's the difference?'

'Clara's an *entraineuse* from our house in Martinique, who's been transferred on three months' probation. Princess Esmeralda's also a new arrival, but came to us from Ethiopia, via the royal concubinery in Trivancore, where she learnt the Indian arts. She declines to work evenings, or without her Nubian companion. Madame Wilson has assigned her the Roman Imperial Bath Suite. When your guest returns, I can tell him you've been postponed.'

Before Worth could formulate his reply, an electric bell sounded. A pair of heavy footsteps passed along the corridor above. The old lady behind the bar slammed shut her book and hurried up the stairs. Worth followed her, fearing the worst.

The door to the *Unter den Linden* Suite at the far end of the corridor, was being opened by a chambermaid. As Worth went towards it, the first voice he heard was a woman's.

'No! You're mad. You'll go to jail.'

There was a thud, and then Snelling saying, 'You're not just a frigging whore.'

Another thud, a sound of splintering, the woman's sob, then Snelling again, 'You're a goddammed German thief.'

The old lady reached the door just ahead of Worth. She glanced quickly back at him. 'Wait outside. I understand these things.'

Worth, following her in, trying to fight down his dread of what, only moments before had seemed a harmless, even a mildly entertaining ploy. What dark spirit was it that Ohio matriarchs fostered in their sons?

The room was amply sized and furnished for its intended purpose, but oddly demure. On an oak bookshelf were leatherbound volumes of the collected works of Kant and Nietzsche. Beneath a false window framing a *trompe-l'oeil* of the Berlin Operaplatz, was a Somalian cane table, and on it, the piano score of Brahms's Ninth Quartet.

A terry robe had been draped over the *cocotte* by the chambermaid. She sat on the bed groaning — from her whitened, uncontorted face, it seemed more with disbelief than pain. Beside her, on the rumpled satin sheet, were the broken remnants of a papier maché chair.

Woth heard himself saying, 'Snelling, what have you done?'

Snelling stood pathetically naked, his beer belly released from the constriction of his trouser belt, his elbows gripped behind his back by the old lady, while the chambermaid snapped a pair of black leather handcuffs around his wrists. He nodded towards the prostitute. 'She knows what she did. Ask her.'

'Fetch Dr Dacre,' the old lady ordered the chambermaid. Then she addressed the woman on the bed. 'What happened, Helga?'

'When I came in from the bathroom, after preparing myself.' Helga's trembling increased as she spoke. 'He'd undressed himself, laid down on top of the bed and gone to sleep. I tried to rouse him, like this.'

She reached out her hand to the level of his groin.

Snelling's agitation erupted again. 'Don't dare touch me. Would you do that to your husband?'

'Please be quiet, Snelling,' said Worth.

'Touch you?' Helga had withdrawn her hand into the folds of terrycloth. 'He woke up and shouted, like he did just now. Then he got off the bed and picked up his suit, as though to get dressed. But he felt in the pockets. And he began to beat me with the chair, so I pressed the alarm.'

Snelling said, 'That whore stole my notebook.'

Worth saw the white-robed house physician standing in the doorway. 'Why should she want your notebook, Snelling?'

Before he could reply, Dr Dacre stepped forward. 'I'll examine you in a moment, Helga,' he said, and spoke to Worth. 'Your friend needs to be calmed. Please assist me.'

He pressed his thumb and middle finger on each of Snelling's jaw joints, forcing open his mouth, into which he deftly inserted a large, hollow rubber wedge. 'So he doesn't bite through his tongue,' the doctor explained.

Worth and Dacre led Snelling to the table, and bent him over it. 'Keep his head down, while I do the necessary,' said the doctor.

Worth pressed his hand against the back of Snelling's neck. Against his own left thigh, he felt the pressure of Snelling's notebook in his trouser pocket.

Dr Dacre was rubbing a small area of Snelling's buttock with alcohol. The patient uttered a low-pitched gurgle. Saliva was dripping on to the Brahms score.

'Try to keep him still for five seconds,' said Dr Dacre. He pierced Snelling's pink skin with the needle of his syringe.

'It's our mission to relieve gentlemen of the burdens of their hidden frustrations,' said Madame Wilson, wizened beyond her years. 'So long as we are informed of them in advance. As Christ is my Saviour, I prohibit little but mock crucifixions. But your disgusting friend . . .'

Her office was a small room at the back of the building. Her small frame was perched on a chair with extra-long legs, behind the marble topped desk. Worth recognised the statuette on it as a terracotta miniature of the couple who stood, entwined, at the entrance to the Sun Temple of Karnak.

He said, 'Much of the blame's mine. I encouraged him to over-indulge at lunch.'

'Who is this Snelling?'

Worth averted his eyes from the gilt-framed Japanese pen drawings on the wall, of the twenty-seven imperial positions. 'He said he's an American detective.'

'Said?' Madame Worth's nostrils narrowed. She took a folder from her desk drawer and looked inside it. 'The Prefect would have sent over a little note, asking me to welcome him personally.'

'I don't think he's the kind of detective Monsieur Lepine mixes with. He claimed he works for Pinkerton.'

'Pinkerton. And you brought him here as your guest?'

Dr Dacre came in without knocking, carrying some papers. In his grave intensity, he seemed not to notice Madame Wilson.

He told Worth, 'You're lucky. Apart from shock, Frau Helga has suffered only minor bruising and five minor skin lesions. I'll send you my bill in a few days. And for your Mr Snelling, the ambulance is already waiting outside the back door.'

Worth looked hard at Madame Wilson, who seemed calmed by the news. Worth felt his own pulse accelerating. 'An ambulance? He didn't need one when I left him.'

Madame Wilson had tensed again. 'What else do you expect? That I call the police here for the first time in fourteen years?'

'It will take him to the St Vitus Hospice for the Insane, in Neuilly,' Dr Dacre explained. 'Does he have any relatives in Paris?'

Worth sat down on the chaise longue, beside an elaborately-boned purple leather corset. 'I understand his family to be in Ohio.'

'Then under French law for the protection of the rights of lunatics, you're his next of kin, and you must pay for his treatment.' Dr Dacre handed Worth the papers he had been holding. 'These are the committal forms. Sign opposite the pencilled crosses.'

Worth ignored the fountain pen proffered by Madame Wilson. 'What'll happen to him?'

'Psychiatric medicine is fortunately more advanced in France than in your country. He will have a room of his own, as comfortable as is consistent with his self-preservation. His case will be supervised by a specialist physician, and he'll be in the immediate care of expert male nurses.'

'Will he receive treatment?'

'Twice a day, he will be strapped to a wooden board, and cold water thrown over him. Each succeeding session drains him, progressively, of his inner hysteria, until he is freed of its grip and becomes himself again.'

'How long is the cure?'

'Until he's fit enough to be de-committed, so Prefect Lepine can sign the deportation order. With skill and God's blessing, as little as a month.'

Worth accepted Madame Wilson's pen, and signed.

8

Worth should have seen the row fermenting in the marital vat on his return from Madame Wilson's. But richly expert though he was in marrying and (he had believed) in untangling himself from such unions, he had little schooling in the disciplines to be followed by a husband in between. Also, he was occupied by the puzzle of Snelling's notes.

'What's it like, going with a French whore?' Angelica asked. 'Is it true they'll kiss your tool but not your lips?'

'It's so long since I did, and so unremarkable, I don't recall.'

'My father used to go on Wednesdays and Fridays.'

'How d'you know?'

'I followed him from his office after the exchange closed.'

'Did you mother know?'

'About him going to the brothel, or about me following?'

'Either.'

'She sensed he did. She didn't need proof.'

There, the unsatisfactory conversation ended, freeing Worth to concentrate on the notebook. Inside its almost new leather covers he counted forty sheets of paper of poor quality; ink applied to them through a nib would blur. The lines were thick and narrow, and the only other printing was on the final page: 'Refills from Central Stationery, Chicago, by Signed Authorisation.'

Snelling's pencil had scrawled its way over five pages. He had written in a curious code, with the exception of one name and address: V. Perugia, 15 Rue de l'Hôpital St Louis — which were spelled out in small, irregular capitals. Perugia's name meant nothing to Worth and presumably, because it was *en clair*, little to Snelling. The address was as lacklustre as any you could find in a petty-crime district of Paris.

He peered at Snelling's pencilled strokes, twirls and curves. They'd been written quickly, so the code did not consist of an alternative alphabet. No human mind could transliterate fast enough to make such a cypher practicable for note-taking. Also, a code of that kind could be cracked by a boy scout with a letter-frequency chart in a children's annual and a free hour.

It had to be a phonetically-based shorthand in which each of the sprawling symbols represented a sound — or a complete word or expression. Worth had taught himself Pitman years before and knew sufficient Gregg to see that Snelling used neither. If the Pinkerton Agency had devised its own confidential shorthand system only its staff could read, Worth would have come across it long ago. His respect for Snelling rose. The phonic hieroglyphics were almost certainly of his own invention; and the only way to decipher them was with the aid of his memory of Sir Isaac Pitman's scale of recurring frequency of the various sound-shapes that make up spoken English.

By three in the morning, he had identified forty-two distinct symbols, which he had copied down the left hand margins of two large sheets of paper. He had hypothetically deciphered eight of them, and was ready to pack in for the night. Before he did, he quickly glanced again along the lines of pencil scrawls. He stopped a quarter of the way down the second page.

Koo. Sells. The two phoneograms blended together in his brain. Coucelles. Henri Coucelles, convicted about three years ago of the theft of Boccaccio's Adoration from the royal chapel of the Chateau of Blois, and convicted to twenty-five years' servitude on Guadeloupe. His escape from the inescapable penal colony had been reported a month ago. With help of the quality that required, by now he could be in Paris. Was Snelling, confined in the insane asylum, still ahead in the race?

Coucelles had had a successful career until Lepine took the train to Blois, sensed his imprint in the chapel, and reasoned with him in the interrogation cell. Dedicated, daring and ungentlemanly though he was, he wasn't, from his record, of sufficient talent to free the Mona Lisa — only to getting far enough to alert the authorities and make the task impossible for Worth. Should he distract himself from his study of the Louvre, to find and neutralise his clumsier competitor?

His brain throbbed dully with fatigue and cigar smoke. Angelica had gone to bed early, saying she felt drowsy. He found her sleepless. She did not reject and she did not respond to him.

Worth woke at half past eleven. He silently shaved and ate an orange.

'We both need to go out,' Angelica said.

He had chosen for their walk the Seine towpath below the south wall of the Louvre. The museum was hidden from their view by a thirty-foot, stone-faced embankment. Angelica was looking at the harnessed shire horse plodding upstream towards them, hauling a paraffin barge. The bargee and his wife sat in the stern on either side of the tiller. He was laughing at what she had just told him.

Worth looked down towards the iron grating set in the gravel path just ahead of them. It was what he'd come here to find. He did not register that Angelica's heel had caught on it until she was falling forwards.

He helped her to the bench and sat beside her. How had he allowed himself to forget that given enough time, a woman becomes an encumbrance?

'Hire me a lady companion and I'll take your damned grand tour,' she said. She rubbed her left ankle.

'Do you think it's fractured, or have you just twisted it?'

She ignored the question. 'Before Lepine kissed my hand, he looked through my eyes into my mind. He saw I'm a criminal. "While in Paris beware of petty theft."'

'He believes everyone to be, particularly himself. Would you prefer your escort to be of the same age, older or younger? Venice, Vienna or Valencia?'

'Worth, it takes two trained men both bigger than you to get the Mona Lisa off the wall. Then you can't get it out of the Louvre. If you do, you can't get it out of the country. They'll be searching for it on every international train, at every border crossing, every port. So what's the point?'

'You didn't ask when you were pleading to remain with me. Besides, you should never trust a man with clear motives. How much monthly allowance do you want to refrain from shoplifting for three months?'

'If you wait in Paris with the painting until the furore dies away, that'll be a long time. Lepine and every policeman in France will be hunting you down, like the French hunt a fox with rabies. The Pinkerton men will arrive to join in, and who knows who else. All that to steal a publicly-owned art treasure in the hope of selling it to the richest man in the world to hide away.'

'Amsterdam, Athens or Algeciras?' Worth asked, and then began to relent. 'Do you think so badly of me, I'd sell it to Morgan?'

She looked towards him for the first time since the row had erupted. There was no more anger in her face. 'I invited myself along, so I've no right to ask why you're doing it. But I've a right to figure for myself. Early this morning, you were running a fever again. I asked how much money we had. You said more than half a million dollars. I asked, "How much more do you need for the rest of your life?" You said, "Not as much." And that's what frightened me.'

She put her hand to his elbow. 'You're out to make a public ass of Lepine. When I saw you together, coming towards the hotel, he looked to me as though he wanted to do the same to you, although he doesn't yet know why.'

'Does what you've said make any sense to you?'

'I wish it didn't. It was like watching a fond reunion between twin brothers who'd been separated in childhood, and who are about to re-find a jealousy and so set out to try to destroy one another. He says a man of your kind he can't outwit doesn't exist. You're frightened that if you don't knock him to pieces first, you might wake up one morning and find him right. That you're not a person, but a series of self-created illusions.'

She turned her head away, as though she was herself taken aback by what she had said. 'What are you going to do?'

'Get the Mona Lisa,' he said, and stood up to look at the iron

96

grating set in the towpath.

It was about a yard wide and two yards long, bolted to a concrete frame which had been set into the gravel. A gust of stale, hot air was rising through it. The odour was neither of sewage nor of Seine flotsam but had a human sourness. It was as though a prostrate giant was beneath, suffering from severe halitosis, except that the flow was constant.

Worth looked over the edge of the steep, concreted river-bank. The tide had half-risen. Parallel with the grating, four feet above the grey river water, he saw the hole.

He took off his jacket and draped it on the bench. He loosened his tie and removed his front collar stud. He knelt with his back to the river, his feet overlapping the towpath's verge.

'Hoist your skirt and get down on your knees facing me. I'm going to hold both your hands tightly, and put most of my weight on to them.'

'Shouldn't we wait till after dark?'

'And attract suspicion?' He progressively backed his legs, from his ankles to his knees, over the rim. He lowered his torso to the path and briefly released his grip on Angelica's hands to reverse it, so that hers were beneath his. He pushed back with his elbows until his hips engaged with the rim. Worth pressed his lower limbs forward against the steep bank, shifting his centre of gravity. As he slid, Angelica lost her grip and his armpits sank from her view.

She grabbed his wrists with an unexpected strength, halting his fall.

With his ribcage squeezed against the concrete, he spoke hoarsely, 'Relax or you'll break my arms, or we'll be in the river. Then in the police infirmary, having our stomachs pumped out.'

His toes felt a ledge, and he moved his feet on to it. Looking down, he could see only that the friction of his body against the sloping bank as he had fallen had pulled his shirt-tails from beneath his trousers on to his chest. He bent his knees forward. They met no resistance. He lowered his hands to the upper lip of the tunnel.

It was about fifty inches in diameter. The roof offered no purchase. Worth crouched forward until his knees were resting on its floor. He pushed his buttocks outwards, over the river, bringing his shoulders level with the rim. He pushed his arms forward, hard against the roof, forced his body to bend, and went into the tunnel, scraping skin from the back of his head.

His body was blocking the aperture, but it was as light as early dusk because of the openings in the iron grating above. He crawled beyond it into darkness. The air was foul, but there was enough oxygen to survive, however unpleasantly. His pupils widened in the gloom, and he saw the tunnel ahead sloping upwards. He crawled on for about thirty yards, then reversed himself back to the grating.

He called through it to Angelica, 'Take off your stockings and lower them over the side.'

He half-climbed, was half-pulled by Angelica, on to the towpath again.

'We've found the exit. Now we'll look for the entrance.'

In a fishing tackle shop on the river bank, Worth bought a trout rod, a tripod, two Starback patent reels with anti-stick metal bearings, a three-pronged hook, artificial bait, two lengths of medium-strength Spanish silkworm gut and a Sheffield clasp knife.

On the towpath above the mouth of the tunnel, he threaded the rod and reel, charged the hook with bait, cast, then placed the rod on its stand.

He wound the other reel with the remainder of the gut — about 180 metres of it — and asked Angelica to put it into her handbag.

As they climbed the stone steps of the embankment, up to the promenade, the Louvre came into view across the road. They were almost opposite the Manège entrance. The Salon Carré, containing the Mona Lisa, was on the floor above, about fifteen yards to the left.

'Look at the chimneys,' he said.

'There's no smoke coming from them. There wouldn't be on a day like this.'

'The angle of the cowlings at the top. If you lit a fire at the bottom, the smoke would be blown straight back down on you. They're wind-towers, to provide a flow of air through the museum. That's why the windows are closed. The tunnel below is the main outlet. It's set into the bank at an angle so the breeze running along the river draws the stale air into itself.'

'So what?'

'Basically, the design is Leonardo da Vinci's. He devised the principle in 1486, as part of his plan to rebuild Milan as a two-storey city. The upper level was to be kept free of traffic and the inferior classes, so that gentlemen could stroll around undisturbed. Workers and vehicles were to be restricted to the lower one. His air-flow system was so that the latter could breathe. It was never used in his lifetime, but Catherine de' Medici had it incorporated into the Louvre when she rebuilt it a century later.'

They had almost reached the Louvre's doorway. Worth said, 'When we're inside, I may without warning press my hand on your elbow, like this. You'll say, just loudly enough for the people nearest us to overhear, "Help me. I'm fainting." Then you'll begin to faint. If it goes as I hope, you'll be helped to a staff rest-room nearby, to recuperate. Insist that you want to be left alone. Once you are, look for — my guess is near the bottom of the wall to the right of the door — a wooden vent, with vertical slats. Measure its width and depth by counting how many lengths of your index finger each of them is. In its centre, there should be a knob which can be moved back and forth, to make the slats wider or narrower. Push it as far as you can in the direction that widens them. Take the fishing reel from your bag. Tie the loose end of the gut once, just once, with a slip-knot, round the bottom of one of the slats, Drop the reel through the vent. Adjust the vent back to where it was before you moved it. Wait two or three minutes. Then come out and tell me you're feeling better but need fresh air.'

'Who is this woman of extraordinary beauty, smiling so enigmatically . . .' The guide was a different one, a pallid woman in her forties, dressed in purple. Not only was the text she recited unvaried by even a word; so was the sensation of chill ennui.

As Worth and Angelica entered the Salon Carré from the south gallery, he saw the door he had remembered, set in the panelling óff the short, wide passageway. Two hundred or more years of use had made it rest in its frame slightly askew. A shadow was cast over it by the back of Titian's vast depiction of the Crucifixion.

A sign with faded gilt lettering, which had been varnished over, stated: 'Accès interdit sauf aux fonctionnaires autorisés.' No entry except to authorised officials. Such a sign, whether in a department store, bank, government building or museum, almost invariably protected a toilet superior to and cleaner than those offered the public, and a row of comfortable chairs.

Near the bottom of the door, two rows of six holes had been drilled.

'. . . Or is the haunting image known to us as Mona Lisa . . .'

'Help me. I'm fainting,' Angelica cried softly. She began to sink sideways, away from Worth, towards two Japanese who were for an instant startled, and then simultaneously took hold of her waist.

'Guard! Come quickly!' Worth called.

He was an elderly man, day-dreaming in the passage leading out to the north gallery. He hurried over, taking as he did so a bunch of keys from his pocket. 'It's forbidden to be ill in the public galleries. Madame must come with me.'

Angelica recovered sufficiently for the old guard to help her to and through the door.

'Sir must wait outside,' the guard ordered, shutting it behind himself and Angelica. About a minute later, he emerged.

'May I go in to her?' Worth asked.

'She asks to be alone.' He was locking the door again. 'When she is ready, she will knock. When she knocks, you will call me.'

The Louvre's defences were starting to crumble with an easy complicity which made Worth wary.

The reel was bobbing in the river, near the mouth of the

tunnel. With his trout rod, Worth hooked it and fished it out. He tugged gently at the gut, which obediently unhitched itself from the staffroom vent above, and Worth wound it in. One hundred and twenty-six metres, allowing for five per cent stretch.

Leonardo's formula for calculating the diameter and downward angle of piping to make his 'Un-mechanical Device for the Provision of Healthy Air' was intended to produce a complete change of air at least every three hours. Stripped of Leonardo's customary mathematical flourishes, the principle was that of correlating minimum predictable wind-speed at the inlets and outlets with the cubic volume of the enclosed space to be aired, to arrive at the amount of boosted velocity to be generated by the design and positioning of the conduits.

'What have we proved?' Angelica asked.

'There are no filters or other obstacles between the vent and this outlet. The approximate difference in height from where we're standing and where Mona Lisa is hanging is twenty-four metres. The length of the piping used for that portion shows its gradient to be as close as makes no difference to Leonardo's formula. At its narrowest— where it passes behind the vent— it's a little over a metre wide. Just enough for a grown man to move around in, uncomfortably.

'As it goes down through the building, and the rubble in the moat into the earth of the embankment and then to here, it gets progressively wider.'

Angelica looked at him with less admiration than he had expected. 'Even if we manage to climb up the conduit — and even if there are iron ladder-rungs, they must have rusted through long ago— not even an infant could crawl through the vent. It's about ten inches high and twenty-three wide.'

Worth lit a cigar. 'It's Mona Lisa who's going out of the Louvre. Once she's stripped of her glass and frame, and the vent cover's removed, there's almost an inch and a half to spare. Leonardo himself's designed the escape route for her.'

'So we just go up to her and say, "Take off thy frame, and walk"?'

'Something like that.'

* * *

Paris closed for lunch between one and three, when all but the restaurants and brasseries were almost deserted. Andrewski the Czech concierge was absent from his glass-hatched cubicle in the entrance lobby of the hotel. Worth and Angelica pressed themselves into the narrow, mahogany-sided elevator.

It reached the fourth floor. Worth opened the gate, and looked across the hallway.

He shut the gate quickly, and pushed the button for the floor above. Beneath the whine of the electrical engine, he asked 'You're certain we locked the door?'

She nodded.

The elevator stopped at the fifth floor. Worth pressed his thumb hard against the red emergency-stop button. The safety-bolt engaged with a metallic click. He snapped off the button and dropped it. 'Follow me downstairs, but not so closely you can't get away if you need to.'

'Who is in there? Why?'

'If we're lucky, the police.'

In the drawing room, with his back to the door, a man stood facing the limewood chest, from which the second drawer had been pulled half-out. He was dressed in a shabby blue serge suit. He was Worth's height, but at least a third broader. He held in his left hand a glass of Worth's best brandy. With his right hand, he was turning over the contents of the drawer.

Worth could have departed as noiselessly as he had arrived. The odds were also excellent of being able to creep up to within three feet of him, and crumple him with a leisurely aimed knuckle punch to the back of his obese neck. Worth could have stayed exactly where he was for as long as it took the man to realise he was there, and then taken advantage of his alarm.

Worth tapped on the parquetry flooring with his shoe heel. An unwilling host, except by showing a degree of tact, was not likely to be told the cause of an uninvited guest's curiosity.

The man turned. He was almost bald. He had very small ears and eyes. His smiling, thick lips were set in a face so flat and powder-grey it might have been starched and ironed.

'Coucelles,' he said. 'I've come for Mr Snelling's notebook.'

'If that's so, why have you broken into my apartment, not Mr Snelling's?'

Coucelles said nothing. His smile was rigid, as though it had been manipulated and sewn into place by a surgeon.

'My acquaintance with Mr Snelling is too slight for him to have visited me here. Had he done so, and left his notebook behind, I'd have sent it round to him. I'm pleased you like my brandy.'

'I've not broken in. I offered the concierge twenty francs to unlock your door with his pass-key. I'd have him sacked. Never trust a Czech.'

'You paid him?'

The smile did not waver. 'He's in your guest-room. With a broken knee-cap, a handtowel stuffed into his mouth, tied up in a pair of sheets, dripping blood on to them. Would you like to come and see?'

'After you've gone.' Worth caught his voice faltering, and forced it back again. 'For an escaped convict, sir, you act indiscreetly.'

His smile seemed to enlarge. 'If they caught me, there's nothing they can do they weren't doing already, beyond a few lashings and some solitary. Please hand me the notebook. Mr Snelling sent me because he wants it particularly.'

There was no discernible escape route except more time. 'If I had it, I'd find your story hard to credit. Mr Snelling is taking therapy at the St Vitus Infirmary and is permitted no visitors.'

'Yes. The orderlies looking after him are my friends. In the penal colony, you get extra rations if you study mental nursing. When you qualify, if the funny-farms are shortstaffed, you can sometimes get remission. The fraternisation break's over. Give me the notebook. I'll take your best painting to save you embarrassment over the concierge, and then I'll go.'

'I don't have it.'

Coucelles was right in front of him. His large hands were clutching Worth three or four inches beneath his armpits. He was lifting him from the floor.

Worth's arms sped forward towards Coucelles's face. Coucelles didn't see them coming, or didn't care, and failed to twist away. Worth's thumbs rammed up into his nostrils, and pressed upwards forcibly, against the fragile flesh.

Water began to ooze from the rims of Coucelles's eyes. He didn't let go. Worth felt his own arms dropping involuntarily and, racing through his chest, a pain more acute than he had known existed.

Coucelles's breathing was almost steady. 'I can press harder. I won't kill you. I'll break your ribcage. You'll be in worse pain than this for three months, every time you move your chest. They'll dose you with morphine for fear if they don't, you'll stop breathing to escape the suffering. By the time they let you out, you'll be an addict. If you'd rather talk about the notebook, blink twice.'

Opening his eyes to prepare for the second blink, Worth saw Angelica. She was standing behind Coucelles. Her hands were partly raised above her shoulders, in parallel. Stretched tightly between them were several thin strands of medium-strength Spanish silkworm fishing-gut. She was lowering them over Coucelles's head, to the front of his neck.

While Worth watched, his eyelids began closing again, and he struggled to reopen them. Coucelles let out a shout, too brief to be a word. The pain in Worth's ribs lessened, and he was falling. His mind filled with a childhood nightmare, of being hurled over Brookline Bridge by black-coated, ring-bearded rabbis.

To his surprise, he was still conscious when his body hit the floor. The back of his head ached fiercely. Coucelles's shout had been the more alarming because it hadn't been of pain, but of stag anger. He was still standing, and his scuffed black boots were turning away.

Worth tried to raise himself, to unbalance Coucelles by jolting his ankles. His limbs refused to move. The lower parts of his legs and arms had been numbed by the rush of blood to his chest.

Brown and blue amoeba shapes drifted back and forth across his vision. Like a kinematographic show beamed through the dusty lens of a jerky, over-heated projector, he saw Coucelles face Angelica. Her hands were struggling to engage the fishing-gut with the base of his ears. His lobes were too small for it to take a purchase, and her hands slipped.

Coucelles dug the tips of his thumb and fingers into the veins on each side of her windpipe.

As she passed out, he increased the pressure, pushing her against the wall with her feet dangling just above the skirting.

He lifted his other hand, to strike her. Worth's limp legs and arms refused to respond to his urgings. He tried to cry out, more from shame than from any hope of preventing the blow. An hour ago, she had asked to leave Paris, him and the Mona Lisa venture; instead, he had drawn her into this living nightmare.

Coucelles flicked a razor from his sleeve and gripped the handle in his palm. The blade was made from bone and was shark-toothed: once it had cut through your skin, the more you struggled, the more you ripped your flesh.

Worth struggled to take in more breath. Pain raced across his chest. With all his remaining will, he forced himself over its threshold. To disfigure a real woman to get at a faded painting of a less beautiful one? He'd abandon Mona Lisa to Pinkertons and Morgan. If Angelica survived this, he'd devote the rest of his and Morgan's money to her — or at least as long as it took to restore her to health and spirit. Worth's vision went black, and he passed out of consciousness.

He could only have been out for a few seconds. Through his aching, uncontrolled eyes, he saw the razor in Coucelles's hand still poised over Angelica. Her head had slumped, and he allowed her to slide to the floor.

Worth found he could move his hand. He did so to signal to Coucelles that he could have the notebook.

Coucelles did not notice. He was staring at the fishing line on the carpet.

Worth managed to emit a croak.

'Be quiet,' Coucelles said. 'I'll see to you next.'

Coucelles dropped his razor and knelt to the floor. Picking up the fishing line, he bent around the first end he found and tied a double-reef to form a small, self-tightening loop. Smiling, he took the other end, and threaded it through. He lifted Angelica's legs, and passed his lasso around them to just below her knees.

Through his right hand, he ran the thread up to the back of her neck, and held it there with a thumb. He wound the line around her neck twice, ran it down again to her knees, and then up to and around her wrists. He tied another double-reef.

He had said nothing to Angelica, and now addressed her through Worth. 'She tried to garotte me. She had no right to do that. I've done nothing any judge could have me executed for. She was trying to take the law into her own hands.'

He stood up. 'Now she can strangle herself while we talk, if she wants. If she tries to free herself by pulling her hands upwards, she'll sever her knee cartiledges. If she pulls downwards, she'll cut into her neck. And if she makes the tiniest sound while we do business, I'll tighten them for her. My friend, you need some of your own brandy.'

Worth felt strength returning on the current of hatred swirling through his aching body. His numbness was fading. His eyes were clearing, and he stared fixedly at Angelica. Her eyes were closed. She was breathing lightly and fast. He tried to fight away remorse; it was too late.

Coucelles brought brandy. He was smiling. Once he had the notebook, he would murder them both and, if he had not forgotten him, Andrewski the concierge.

If surrender meant death, what possible strategy of resistance was there? He employed his voice with undisguised effort. 'You learnt that at the school of mental nursing?'

'My uncle taught me when I was a kid in the Marais. We used to do it to rich boys, after we robbed the brothel money their mothers gave them to prevent them masturbating.'

Coucelles was more dangerously composed than he had been before his exhilaration. His hand was calm and steady as he gently passed the glass into Worth's.

Worth raised it four or five inches, then let it slip through his fingers and smash on the floor.

'You're still too feeble. I'll bring you another in a while.'

Coucelles glanced down. 'My friend, your brandy's stripping the polish from your parquetry. I'll clear it up. Otherwise your wife will be cross with us.'

From the kitchen he brought a linen dishcloth on which had been printed the image of Mona Lisa, and a small, long-handled pot-brush. He bent down and with careful strokes swept the pieces of glass on to the cloth. When he was satisfied all the fragments and splinters were inside, he neatly folded the cloth twice and wiped the floor with it. He straightened himself, and went back to the kitchen. Worth heard the parcel being dropped into the rubbish chute. He could move now, and did not.

'No more to worry about. The stain on the parquetry's very small. Unless she counts her cloths, she'll never realise. Give me Mr Snelling's notebook, and I'll go. Then when you're well enough, if you want to, you can cut her free. I've two of those razors. I'll leave one.'

'I don't have the notebook.'

'That's where our disagreement started. Shall I squeeze your chest again or this time break your leg? What's all the paper-work in your study? Who're you working for?'

'In this hotel suite I don't have it.' Worth felt his lungs ready to expand through the next pain barrier. He held them back. 'You and I are working for the same man, Snelling's just the runner. How much do you want to move off the pitch?'

'They sprang me from Guadaloupe to do a job. I'll do it, not you.' Coucelles was speaking with the frankness of a man who knows his listener won't survive beyond the conversation.

Worth took a slightly deeper breath. 'Who's Perugia?'

Coucelles looked at him, silently admitting the question unsettled him, but not knowing how.

'It's in the notebook. V. Perugia, 15 Rue de l'Hôpital St Louis. I took him to be your partner, seeing it takes two strong men to lift the painting.'

Coucelles said nothing.

'Snelling seems to be offering the job around town. I suggest you and I together push Perugia aside.'

Coucelles was relieved by the desperate implausibility of the offer. 'Where's the notebook?'

'In my room at the Press Club.'

Coucelles laughed and shook his head. 'You're the kind of crook I don't like. I already looked there.'

'In the little drawer in the base of the telegraph transmitter? Tie me up. Leave me here while you go and find it. If it's not there, you'll know where to find me.'

Coucelles perceived a ruse. 'We'll leave your wife where I'll know to find her, and you'll come with me. If you try to raise the alarm, I'll slash off your balls from behind and get away, before anyone's hardly realised you've shouted. And you know it's true.'

Worth nodded in genuine agreement.

In the hallway outside, Worth pressed the call button for the elevator. He paused for some moments. The car remained stationary on the floor above. He grasped the door handle.

Supposedly, the elevator had been designed in accordance with the principles of Elisha Otis, so that the outer door remained firmly locked until released by a ratchet jutting from the side of the arriving car. But beneath the handle a small, recessed lever had been concealed, for the convenience of maintenance engineers. Worth pushed it up with his thumb while pulling the handle down with his fingers.

He opened the door several inches. 'Would you like me to go first, or to follow you?'

Worth could feel Coucelles close behind him, half to one side. 'We'll go together.'

That's all too probable, Worth thought, transferring his hand from the outside to the inside handle, swinging the door wide open.

Coucelles saw the emptiness. He grabbed hold of the back of Worth's collar and thrust him forward.

Worth dipped his slender frame, so that the impetus would thrust Coucelle's bulk over him, head-first into the chasm. The collar of Worth's jacket ripped away in Coucelles's hand and Coucelles remained where he was.

Worth had failed to compensate quickly enough for the sudden release of pressure. He felt his feet slipping forwards until the insteps of his shoes caught on the ledge.

Coucelles's fist smashed down on Worth's clutch on the door handle. There was a knee-jab piercing through to the nerves in the base of his spine. He tried to hold what remained of his balance. The fist smashed down a second time on to his hand on the handle, and its muscles gave way. Worth was falling.

Most fractures of the wrist are caused by an irresistible impulse to put out your arm to protect yourself in a fall which might otherwise leave you uninjured. Worth's uninjured hand hit the cable dangling down from the elevator car locked into place above. His fingers closed round it.

The heels of his shoes still held against the ledge. Coucelles coughed.

Three floors below them, someone was rapping against the elevator shaft's steel walling. 'Either come down in it or release it.'

To call for help from such a distance would make death more certain. Fashionable physicians — those who listen to their patients instead of submitting them to medical examination — diagnosed fear of falling as an emotional ailment they termed vertigo, for which they prescribed small doses of cocaine solution.

Peering down an empty elevator shaft, even in the most favourable circumstances, the cause did not seem to be necessarily neurotic; but neither was it entirely rational. The laws of three-dimensional perspective, first formulated by Leonardo da Vinci and little revised since, seemed to function only horizontally. To see how deceitful 'three-dimensional vision' was on the vertical plane, an unclothed woman had only to look down on her breasts, or a man at his lower protuberance. Even with the best-aligned, clearest-sighted pair of eyes, there tends to be a grotesque distortion. Looking down through his one serviceable eye into the lowering gloom, he saw — ninety feet? two hundred feet? thirty feet? — below, the glistening steel safety-piston looming up towards him, to impale him.

'Revenge isn't my nature,' Coucelles said from behind. 'But your skull instead of mine is. I won't kick your heels away. It'd be slower, but you'd go down feet first.'

Another burst of sharp knocking on the gate three floors down. 'Stop talking up there and send the elevator. The shops are reopening.'

Worth heard Coucelles spread his feet to either side of his, and felt approaching warmth from his body as he leaned forward into the shaft above him. 'Turn your head up and look at me.'

Coucelles had taken a single-hand grip on the cable — eighteen inches? — above Worth's grasp of it. His other hand held the shark-toothed razor. He swung it across the edge of Worth's line of vision, then it bit into the cable's thick rubber sleeve, and Coucelles began to saw.

'The notebook's still underneath the telegraph machine?'

'No.'

'You're a fibber. Has your wife got it?'

The voice from below called up, 'I'm calling the concierge to make a formal complaint.'

Coucelles sawed back and forth. 'I won't get a shock. The handle's bone. The notebook?'

The strain of Worth's back, now at a thirty degree angle to the abyss, had nearly become unendurable.

His knees were giving way.

'I'm summoning the manager,' said the voice from below.

'Please. Only a few more seconds now,' Coucelles called back. Afterwards, he could climb the stairs to the attic, and exit across the roof.

Worth's heels slipped from the ledge. His bruised hand went out and painfully clutched the cable. As it bent forward below the cut under his weight, he raised his legs and kicked against the opposite wall with all his adrenalin-driven force.

There was a metallic clang and the cable began to swing backwards. He speeded it with a second kick and braced his spine and buttocks for the collision.

Coucelles's legs must still have been apart; for as Worth's body swung through the doorway, it hit the insides of his attacker's knees.

Worth let go of the cable and hunched his trunk. The sole of his left shoe caught a purchase on the edge of the door-frame. He gripped the ledge with his bruised right hand, and pushed his trunk beneath Coucelles's legs.

Coucelles was still leaning forward, gripping the cable above the cut in one hand, his razor in the other. Worth tugged at his ankles to topple him, but he was too weak and Coucelles too heavy.

Coucelles was working his grip on the cable slowly downwards towards the incision he had made in it, so his other hand could get near enough to Worth to slash at him with the razor. Worth's hand reached up to the apex of his legs, found and sharply pulled at his testicles.

Coucelles hand slipped suddenly on the cable and stopped at the incision. The shaft lighted with a blue and yellow flash of 220 volts finding a human earth.

Temporarily blinded, Worth tugged himself backwards as Coucelles collapsed and then toppled forwards.

It was said by some who had been near to it that the potential reward of resignation to sudden death is an instant of unique tranquility, free of disturbing memories.

As Coucelles fell head-first down the narrow shaft, towards the steel piston, he uttered a scream Worth had never before heard from the mouth of a human being.

'I am not asking. I'm telling,' said Andrewski the concierge. 'I know my French legal rights. A public investigation by the magistrate with me giving evidence.'

Coucelles' body had been wrapped in canvas and hauled from the bottom of the shaft by municipal sanitary workers, two of whom — North Africans — had stayed on to scrub the walls with disinfectant. Angelica, cut free, sat in an upright chair, wrapped in Worth's bathrobe. For the first time in her life she was trying to smoke a cigarette, given her by the police sergeant. It increased her trembling, and she put it out. Andrewski's knee, as far as Worth could tell from his probing of it, had at worst a hairline fracture.

'Concierge,' the police sergeant said. 'If you want, I'll go and fetch you a litre of hundred-proof vodka, bought with my own money. I'll get your picture published in the afternoon papers. I'll recommend you for the Prefect's Certificate of Civic Heroism. But you've no rights. You're a foreigner. There's too much serious crime for us to investigate an accidental death of an escaped convict.'

Worth thought it imprudent not to protest. 'I'm a foreign correspondent accredited to your government. He assaulted and bound Mr Andrewski. He trussed and nearly killed my wife. He almost murdered me. He said he belonged to a gang of professional art robbers. We insist on police protection.'

'If he told you, it's not to be believed. Do you write pro-German articles?'

'None about politics.'

'Then I can't recommend you for protection. It's reserved for journalists who write anti-French articles, and we're over-stretched. You'll have to hire yourself a guard from Pinkertons.'

'Can we have a doctor?' Angelica asked.

'Would you like a regular doctor or an unlicenced one?'

'Are the others cheaper?'

'They charge more because of the fines they have to pay. The unlicenced ones do things the regulars aren't allowed. Click your spine back into place. Supply you medicines that aren't on the approved list. So you get better quicker. When me or my colleagues get roughed up, we use Dr Tang.'

'What commission does he pay you for introductions?'

'Same as the regular doctors. Twenty-five per cent.'

Dr Tang, despite his name, looked more Cambodian than Chinese. He worked with his small hands, first on Angelica, then on Worth.

Worth asked, 'Do you have any sedative you could leave us?'

'I'll put some paper screws of mushroom powder on the chest of drawers. Infuse them in hot water and drink. It will help you forget.'

The assistant hotel manager who came into the suite wore striped trousers and a black tail coat, and was deeply em-barrassed. 'The director has asked me to convey his regrets. The concierge has been dismissed.'

He paused. Worth didn't help him.

'He also suggests, after what's happened, you'd feel out of place remaining in the Plaza-Athénée with our other guests. There's no question of us presenting your bill. May I send the maids to help you pack?'

'Yes,' Worth replied. 'Tomorrow.'

'Venice?' Angelica asked. They lay in bed uncovered in the night heat, his arm around her shoulders, her hand on his breast. 'How can you talk of leaving Paris after a day like this?'

V. Perugia 15 Rue de l'Hôpital St Louis.

It was almost six o'clock. The Café Jupiter's breakfast coffee had been brewed long before, mostly from essence of chicory, and was as bitter as the proprietor who grudgingly poured it from his chipped enamel jug.

'You already had yours,' he said when Worth asked for another cup. He was in his mid-thirties, with black stubble on his face and a hangover. His word order was un-French, his accent nasal Québecois.

Worth replied silently, by placing a five-centime coin beside his empty cup on the dented zinc counter.

In France, the later you got out of bed, the higher your social rank. On this, the second day of his convalescence, Worth had left the solace of the four-poster in the balconied apartment they had rented on Boulevard Montmarte at half past four, to reach the Rue de l'Hôpital St Louis in time for the local reveille.

As he had climbed the rattling iron stairs to the pedestrian gangway over the rail-tracks north of the Gare du Nord, the pain in his chest sharpened again. Any cab driver who knew Rue de l'Hôpital St Louis refused to take you there, even for double the meter. This was not merely for the passenger's own welfare, though it was the kind of street in which to be seen alighting from a taxi was almost a provocation in itself. It was the southern border of *L'Enclave des Peaux Rouges*, the Red Indian Reservation.

Worth had turned from the factories lining Avenue Leprieure, down the road past the Jacob family's burnt-out canvas mill, and on to the bridge over the Canal St Martin. The chest pain had subsided. His eyes directed his legs' still aching tendons towards the shop fronts on the far bank. Agadir Halal Butchery. Piccadilly Gin and Ale Palace. Salonika Confectionery. San Diego Japanese Steam Laundry. Minsk Steambath and Birch-twig Massage House.

Few Parisians ventured any further, except possibly on Sunday afternoons to visit a parent in St Louis Hospital, staffed by Pondicherry nuns recruited as virgin child-widows in India, and one of the less expensive places in town to linger before death. Foreign tourists glimpsed L'Enclave through the five-centime telescopes on the top platform of the Eiffel Tower, and moved on quickly to more interesting views before the coin dropped.

L'Enclave contained no native Americans, and was as empty of women and children. Yet it was not, as many assumed, a slum district. The slum had been flattened by municipal steam engines six years before. The municipality had then run out of money to replace them with modern grey-slab tenements. So the plots had been staked by the quarter's Armenian and Egyptian money lenders, who had had their debtors build— in return for partial write-offs of their debts— rows of two-storey post-and-beam, plaster-boarded lodging houses. The money-lenders then rented out the rooms to the men who had built them.

'No more coffee,' said the Québecois behind the bar. 'You're intimidating my customers.'

Worth looked round. Apart from himself and the owner, the café was deserted. Only one table had been laid, with six saucerless cups, six chunks of bread and six lengths of garlic sausage. 'I'm the only customer, and there's my money.'

The Café Jupiter was at the corner of Chemin Colbert and Rue de l'Hôpital St Louis. Through the misted window, Worth saw six men come out of the doorway of number fifteen.

The proprietor said, 'You look like an immigration *flic*.'

Worth's coin had disappeared from the counter. 'Am I dressed like one? I'm not even French.'

'Nor are the *flics*.'

The six men were crossing the street together, towards the café. None of them was yet middle-aged. Their hair was short-cropped and they were clean-shaven. Their blue dungarees had been washed and pressed.

Worth put a twenty-franc note on the zinc.

The proprietor glanced at it, and to the approaching men. 'Who are you looking for?'

'Perugia.'

'You're the second American detective to come in here for him this week.' The twenty-franc note had been spirited from the counter.

'Go through the bead curtains into the back room and I'll bring him to you when he arrives.'

'Tell him I'm not a detective. I'm an art critic.'

The men were near to the entrance of the café.

'My father-in-law's a journalist too. He's why I left Montreal,' said the proprietor. 'Just leave your revolver behind the bar.'

'I've no gun.'

'I'll sell you one of mine before you leave. You need one around here.'

The café's door was opening.

Worth did not linger in the back room. Though he could hear no voices from the café, he had no spare time, while the proprietor warned Perugia to take his breakfast custom elsewhere. He left quietly through the rear exit and hurried over the soggy earth of the passageway to the cobbled side-alley. He saw a man coming out of the café, turn left and then right.

Perugia's detour through the streets of tenements and workshops to the Gare du Nord was not a lengthy one. He turned his head twice, and the second time saw Worth.

He slowed his pace, to give Perugia more distance. Perugia maintained his, and did not look back again. It was a myth that nervous men, when they first suspected they were being followed, broke into a run. Their bodies stiffened visibly, and their gait taughtened. Perugia's was steady, as though he was resigned to being trailed.

At the station he boarded the 62 motor-omnibus. He was not as impoverished as his neighbours, who used the horse-trams, or at least did not expect to be so for long.

Worth waited while three more passengers boarded and did so himself. He sat across the car from Perugia, facing him at right angles. His quarry did not acknowledge him. He had a Siennese-brown, unlined complexion and the angular face of the sixteenth-century aldermen whose portraits hung in Tuscan town-halls.

Perugia left the bus in Rue de Rivoli and he walked, still steadily, in the same direction for about a hundred and fifty yards. He went through a small doorway in the north wall of the Louvre.

V. Perugia left the museum by the same door at six in the evening. He walked along the Rivoli's colonnaded pavement for almost sixty paces, slowly. Other blue-dungareed, sullen labourers who came out with him hurried past him on both sides. He stopped at the window of Laferre et Fils, dealers in Renaissance art, and half-turned, waiting for Worth to come alongside.

'You follow me again. What do you want?'

The manner was mild and puzzled.

If only Worth knew the answer. 'You seemed to prefer it to a meeting in the Jupiter.'

'Who sent you?'

'Mr Snelling.'

'I'm not important enough for him to come himself?'

'He's ill in hospital, and particularly asked me to find you.'

'How am I to know he's not in jail? That you're not a *flic*?'

'By now, I'd have you for suspicious conduct. Cross the street and we can talk in the open.'

The Tuileries extended west of the Louvre to the Place de la Concorde. Though the French called it a garden, it struck the foreign eye as being more akin to a parade-ground. Its twenty acres of raked gravel were without flowers, but were interspersed with iron-fenced lozenges of grass, which the summer's sun and drought had bleached light brown.

On one of these, a man dressed as a cossack was playing a concertina. Handcuffed to his left wrist was a bear with moth-eaten fur, who danced clumsily to the tune.

Almost half-way through *There will always be our Tsar*, the bear became tired and lost the rhythm. The accordionist faltered, then polkaed backwards and tapped the rear of her ankle with his toe-cap.

The bear froze, became motionless. Still playing his accordian, the cossack swung back his heel to administer a kick. His boot met the shin of a gendarme approaching him from behind.

The gendarme swore, and bent to rub the nascent bruise. Panicking, the Russian attacked him with a sharp right-hook of his boot to his achilles tendon. The gendarme fell. The man and his beast began to run heavily away together. Worth heard the Russian shout angrily to the bear what sounded to be, '*Gobtuyu! Mat!*'

'It's what Russians say when they're upset,' observed V. Perugia. 'It means bugger your mother. The man thinks they'll be put on the deportation train to Minsk. Then he'll be sent to a hard-labour camp for insulting the dignity of Holy Russia.'

'It seems a restrained enough remark in the circumstances.'

In a delayed reaction, the incident triggered the impatience Perugia thus far had concealed. 'Have you brought the photos?'

Photographs? Worth quickly took in Perugia's expression. 'Mr Snelling did pass them to me, with the negatives. I studied them carefully. . .'

Perugia's eyes flinched. 'Sir, I don't really prefer men. But since my fiancée left me . . . In L'Enclave, one takes what one can get, so long as there's money in it.'

'After I studied them, I observed you this morning and concluded that Mr Snelling had misunderstood you. A momentary lapse, a single slip, and a man's life can be in ruins. So I have burnt them.'

'How can I know? Mr Snelling promised their return.'

'Mr Snelling hasn't been quite himself. As I'll explain to him when he's recovered, it's in our interest, as well as yours, that you should be free for the moment from fear of the authorities.'

'And afterwards?'

'Mr Snelling will be counting on your discretion all the more. News you'll find less welcome is that he's decided your fee is too high.'

'Sir, two thousand francs is very little for an employee pass card to the Louvre.'

Worth swallowed against a suddenly dry throat. 'He's concerned about the problem of recognition. He does not look at all like you.'

'He knows there's no photo on the card, only your right thumb print. As I told him, I've been working there over a year. I've yet to see one checked.'

'The security guards know you.'

'They're French, in blue and gold uniforms. I'm a better painter than some of the French artists whose works they've got hanging in fat gilt frames in there. But I'm an Italiano, one of the foreign skivvies in dungarees. They look at our passes, not our faces.'

'Your foreman knows you.'

'I've already been through this with Mr Snelling.'

'Mr Snelling means no offence, but there's a lot of money at stake. He asked me to go through it again with you, to double-check.'

'Labourers are always quitting and being sacked and new ones hired. You don't work under one foreman. In the morning, we stand in line in the yard and the Chief-Ganger numbers us off from the right into duty platoons of eight men each. We don't know each other's names. Most can only speak a few words of French.'

'If only he could have heard you, Mr Snelling would have been reassured. Let's agree a financial compromise.'

Perugia stopped pacing the gravel a few feet from a plane tree, whose shrivelled leaves were already beginning to drop two months ahead of autumn. The day's fierce sun had become a glowing red ball, sinking towards the distant silhouette of the Arc de Triomphe. Worth leant his nagging body against the treetrunk.

'Compromise? They won't compromise with me. How can I with you?' He took from his pocket a worn moroccan wallet and from it, a ragged newspaper clipping which he unfolded and handed to Worth.

It was a wordy advert, torn from *La Nazione* of Florence.

Worth handed it back to him. 'My Italian is indifferent. What does it say?'

'That if you're an Italian artist, you can make thousands of dollars a month in the USA, painting the portraits of beautiful women. Commissioned by their husbands.'

Worth rubbed his back. 'What qualifications do they require?'

Perugia looked at the clipping. 'Four hundred years ago, it was the Medicis of Florence. Today, it's New York's princes of finance who want to bestow their lavish patronage on painters of promise, like you. Any extra training you need will be provided after you arrive, by a European Grand Master.'

Worth asked, 'You believe that?'

'It's in the newspaper,' Perugia replied. 'They also give you a studio in the fashionable artists' colony of Bronx, an easel and all your paints and materials.'

Worth watched a girl — perhaps seventeen — pause, to allow her mongrel dog to urinate on the gravel. 'How do you get clients?'

'They almost do it for you. They provide a secret list of twenty-five names and addresses of New York millionaires, and a sample of the letter you copy out and send to them.'

'What else does the advertisement say?'

Perugia ran his fingers through his short hair, and looked boldly into Worth's eyes. 'That you have to send $399.99 to Renaissance Master Painters Inc. care of Agencia Lorenzo, Post Box 618, Genoa, Italy. For that you get everything they say, plus your steamship passage and a valuable twenty-four page book called: *Ellis Island – What to Tell (And Not to Tell) US Immigration Officers*. In Italian.'

They were close to a deal. Worth said, 'Four hundred dollars isn't two thousand francs. It's twelve hundred.'

Perugia took from his pocket another piece of paper, with sums written on it. 'There's the back rent I owe Mr Mounarian. Your life's not worth living if he sees you trying to leave without paying, and I have to take my trunk of paintings with me. Then there's the train fare to Genoa, and Francesca's passage is an extra forty-nine dollars. When we get to New

York, we'll need to live. Millionaires are busy men. It might take them two weeks or more to write back to me.'

'Is Francesca your wife?'

'My fiancée. If I get the money, she'll run away with me. Give it to me now, and I'll give you the pass. Mr Snelling's to be at the museum by seven in the morning. What he'll do in there'll be none of my business. I'll take tonight's train from Gare du Sud and be in Genoa by then.'

He misjudged Worth's hesitation. 'Before I go, I can show you how to handle heavy paintings without assistance. They tell people it can't be done without two strong men. It's a bluff. They taught me how to do it alone. Luckily for Mr Snelling, I'm not good at keeping secrets.'

Worth raised his back from the tree, and began to walk with Perugia towards Place de la Concorde. 'Here's a hundred francs. You're to report to work tomorrow as normal. The remainder will be paid to you in instalments, as you follow instructions. After work, you're to go to your lodgings, pay Mr Mounarian, collect your paintings and meet me in the Place de Tertre at eight-thirty.'

'What'll I tell them in L'Enclave?'

'That you've landed your first commission as a portraitist, for two thousand francs, and you're moving to an artist's atelier in Montmartre.'

'They won't believe me.'

'It's the truth.'

Up. Two, three. Almost an inch gained. Hold and rest; two thousand, three thousand, four thousand, five thousand. Another half-inch, and it would clear the wall hooks. Push up again. Two and *three*.

The slim wooden box did not move. Its dimensions were similar to the Mona Lisa's, and its interior was lined with a hundred and thirty pounds of lead. Typically of Snelling's dealings with the rest of humanity, there were many unsatisfactory aspects to his arrangement with Perugia which would require close and continuing attention. One which could be avoided was trusting in his discretion over passing on the technique of lifting a heavy painting single-handed. If Perugia had been successfully tutored to do it, Worth could surely deduce the method, and teach himself.

He leant forward, pressing the box against the bedroom wall with his hands, to prevent it slipping again. The money Snelling had agreed to pay for the pass was far too little compared with the rewards that would be offered by the Government afterwards for its return. It seemed the more inadequate when you put into the balance the naïveté of a blackmail threat over sodomy in Paris in 1911. Despite the statutory penalties, Lepine's celibate attitudes towards sexual aberrations in others was one of detached fascination; and it was fast becoming known that his disgust and retribution were directed to the blackmailer when it was not himself and he was not plea-bargaining.

Up. *Two*, three. A quarter of an inch maybe. Hold, rest and think. You could give Perugia enough money for Francesca's train fare, so she could join him in his atelier in Montmartre, then ship them both off from Cherbourg on a slow ocean liner to New York. That would leave you in Paris, holding the cancelled pass of a Louvre employee who'd gone missing from his residence. You could pay him to resign, turn in his pass to the Louvre authorities, then devise a new face and apply to the Louvre for his job. When the theft was discovered, you as a new recruit would be among the first suspects.

Up. Two and three. Two-thirds of Mona Lisa's total weight was in the frame and the protective glass. Once off the wall, they'd be easy to discard. The *Vade Mecum of Museum Administration*, completed by Dr A. Apoineau four years after his retirement as Director of the Louvre, said the one reliable method of securing a painting on a wood-block was with six-centimetre iron flanges screwed into and projecting from the rear of the frame. Four were sufficient. Worth put his left shoulder beneath the box, and suddenly straightened his legs.

Up, up, *up*. The box cleared the hooks. Worth felt a jolt of pain in his lower spine and dropped the box.

At eight-thirty, Perugia was standing with his trunk at the

north-west corner of the Place de Tertre, the furthest away from the church of the Sacred Heart. Whatever he had had to pay Mr Mounarian, there had been enough over for a blue pin-stripe cotton suit, a silk shirt and a Belgian cravat.

'How did you recognise me?' he asked Angelica.

'Mr Snelling told me to look for a man like Leonardo da Vinci.'

'Has he sent you with the money?'

'Some, for starting the portrait. He told me to take you to your atelier.'

The studio Worth had rented for three-months' money down was on the top floor of Bateau Lavoir, 13 Rue Ravignon. It was not the cheapest attic room in Montmartre, and lacked electricity or running water. The rent reflected the rundown building's new cachet. The great art-dealer Kahnweiler, touring its near cubicles almost on impulse after a heavy lunch a year ago, had discovered Picasso and paid him in cash there and then for his existing stock twenty times more than he had earned in the previous ten years.

Picasso had spent the money moving himself, his mistress Fernande and their adopted daughter Célice to a furnished apartment on the Boulevard with two bathrooms, a roof-garden and a grand piano none of them knew how to play.

Angelica had been there with Worth for Henri Rousseau's eightieth birthday party, given by Picasso at Kahnweiler's expense. Ex-neighbours from the Bateau Lavoir had not been invited. An art critic in Kahnweiler's pay, Wilhelm Apollinaire, had told an American punter, Gertrude Stein, that she was akin to an anus surrounded by a ring of thorns, and had been expelled. Célice, six years old, had left the room to be sick and had done so over the hat of Miss Stein's companion, Alice Toklas. Chosen by barren Fernande from a convent orphanage because of their shared detestation of boiled spinach, Célice was locked up for the night. It was rumoured that next day Fernande tried to return Célice to the convent. The nuns refused to have Célice back. Fernande took her to Guy Salmon, who was a bachelor literary journalist and also an orphan, with a reputed interest in young girls.

At Bateau Lavoir, rooms which were rented for eight francs a month when Picasso was there fetched fifteen a week from artists waiting for Kahnweiler to make a return visit.

The walls were yellow and the distemper was peeling. Worth had furnished it with artist's materials and little else. Perugia stood on a bare floorboard which was springy from the damp fungus beneath. 'When do I go to Bronx?' he asked.

Angelica sat on the bed, looking through his trunkful of paintings. The bed had a frayed and unyielding hay mattress. The seven paintings were of abysmal quality. 'Do you always paint naked women?'

One was squinting at two red roses with bruised petals in a cracked glass jar; another was simultaneously weeping and smiling. Between the breasts of the seventh, a small spider was weaving a web.

'They say it's what the millionaires want to buy. When Leonardo sold the Mona Lisa to the King of France, she had bare breasts. It was the Queen who had the bodice painted over. The two roses are me and my fiancée. The spider is her father.'

Angelica began to take off her clothes.

'There's no lock on the door, no curtains,' said Perugia. The only vertical window was on to a small courtyard, and was overlooked from the other side.

'We don't want neighbours to think this is a social visit,' Angelica said, peeling off her other stocking. 'Mr Snelling's paying both of us to act professionally. If it'll make you feel easier, get undressed yourself.'

'If that's what you're after, I'll have to explain,' he said. 'She isn't Francesca. He's Francesco.'

'You get to seem more and more like Leonardo da Vinci,' she replied, unbuttoning her camisole. 'He had to go abroad for the same reason. Do you think that when a great artist dies, his soul lives on in a successor? Some people say the Mona Lisa's face is actually that of his boyfriend, Salai. Why's the Louvre closed to the public on Mondays?'

'Some of us work in the library, putting back the folios and manuscripts the curators and students have taken off the shelves during the week. Some of us are sent up to the photographers' gallery, to go and fetch the paintings they want to copy. Then we play poker in the staff room until the pictures are ready to be taken back down again.'

'You just lift a painting from its hooks and carry it away?'

'Obviously not. You must hang the docket where the painting was. A piece of cardboard saying, "TEMPORARILY REMOVED FOR REPRODUCTION." Otherwise the guards go crazy.'

'I'll come back for a second sitting tomorrow. Bring one of those cards,' said Angelica, beginning to dress rapidly. 'You're so handsome, no wonder Francesco's in love with you.'

Worth's trousers and shirt were removed by Dr Tang, who had eased him on to the carpet, face down.

'*Fu wan*,' the doctor remarked sombrely, to himself. He stood and, balancing first on one foot then the other, removed his shoes and socks with an easy agility Worth, watching from the floor, found tantalising. Dr Tang soaked his handkerchief in sour-smelling alcohol from a brown bottle and rubbed his soles with it.

'Do not be alarmed,' he said.

Two short steps and he was standing between Worth's shoulder blades, one either side of his vertebrae. Slowly and steadily, he rocked his feet backwards and forwards, his toes exploring and kneading each spinal disc, his heels pressing rhythmically against the surrounding muscle, moving towards the small of Worth's back.

'For God's sake, stop.' Worth could not move.

'A French doctor would confine you to bed, on a plank, for one month.' Dr Tang's feet continued their progress.

Worth felt he was being stabbed in the base of his spine. Dr Tang shifted his balance and jumped. As he landed, there was a crackle of bone shifting position, and the pain decreased.

'Tomorrow, you can dance with your wife the polka,' said Dr Tang, replacing his footwear. The claim seemed implausible, but so was the effect of the treatment so far. 'What did you do?'

Worth turned on his side and pointed to the box on the wall. 'I was trying to lift it down.'

The doctor stepped over him, put his hands beneath the box, and pushed upwards. It did not move. 'Why is it here?'

'It's an English exercise device, for strengthening the upper torso and limbs.'

'You are English?'

'No.'

'They are masochists. Show me the instructions.'

'There aren't any. It's part of the challenge. You have to figure it out yourself.'

'What's inside?'

'Lead.'

Dr Tang stared silently at the box for over a minute. 'Permit me to roll you out of the way.'

His back to Worth, his fingers pointing outwards, he pressed his palms against each side of the box, two-thirds of the way down. His shoulder and arm muscles tightened. His back seemed to relax, as he bent his knees. He was breathing more rapidly. The palms of his hands were flattened against the box as far as they could go, blue veins standing up from the skin.

'*Ah Choy!*' His hands remained in place. With a sudden tensing of his thighs, his legs straightened, and the box slid about four inches up the wall with a grating sound.

Dr Tang looked down at his feet. The force of his exertion had shifted them a little backwards and further apart. He meticulously returned first the right, then the left, to their previous positions.

Keeping his arms fully extended, he relaxed his wrists, allowing the top of the box to lean away from its hooks. To prevent it from sliding out of control, he alternately clutched and relaxed his fingers as it slowly descended to the two-thirds mark. He restored his grip, and bent his knees as it went smoothly down to the floor.

Dr Tang turned. 'Thought, not strength. I am leaving you more paper twists of mushroom powder by your bedside. Follow the directions as before. It will help you both forget your problems.'

*　　*　　*

It was the end of the first full week in August. Paris was shutting down for the rest of the summer. Each day, as the temperature rose higher, the crowds of Parisians in the streets thinned. Side-street shops and cafes had signs in their windows, 'Reopening September'. Increasingly, only those which catered to foreign visitors and charged a fifth or a quarter more, remained open.

At midday on Friday, the shaded thermometer in St Maur Park recorded one hundred and three degrees Fahrenheit—the highest temperature of the century. The Public Utility Authority announced that for the duration of the drought, supplies of water to residential buildings would be limited to two hours each morning and evening. Prime Minister Caillaux announced that the negotiations for détente with Berlin had been postponed by mutual agreement until autumn, when Parliament would be recalled. He left for his chateau in Normandy, though his wife remained behind on private business.

The bathing pool in the Bois de Boulogne was open to customers, though almost deserted. Worth and Angelica, in swimming costumes, picnicked beside it under the shade of a lime tree. He had completed the dose of swimming prescribed by Dr Tang. Aspic around the *oeufs en gelée* was melting. The *jambon persillé* was sweating. The *filets de truite fumée* were curling inwards. The *champignons à la grecque* had drowned in their marinade. The white wine was tepid. Worth raised his eyes and saw a glistening drop of sweat fall from Angelica's cheek.

'How long before we do it?' she asked.

Worth had no appetite, and unwrapped a Siamese cheroot. 'Perhaps another week. Everything's been moving in our favour now.'

'But you're uneasy.' She bit a stalk of yellowing asparagus.

'So far, it's been too easy. There'll never be another theft on this scale until Leonardo da Vinci has a second coming and paints another Mona Lisa.'

Angelica picked a daisy from the grass and dropped it into his wine goblet. 'I didn't think you to be superstitious.'

'Recently, I've been having a nightmare — not a dream. Just after I wake in the morning. I'm acting in a play. The script's already been written. Only the producer knows what's in the rest of it, and you and I can't change it.'

On the way back to their apartment, the taxi passed a newspaper placard. 'MASS JAIL BREAK-OUT IN AMERICA.'

'A week's the most we've got,' said Worth.

In the attic room at 13 Rue Ravignon, Angelica found Perugia, red-eyed from crying, dressing himself. 'Take the pass and the photographer's docket for a thousand francs,' he said pointing to them on the table. 'I'm going.'

'You're ill. You are going straight back to bed.'

He looked at her defiantly, and put on his shirt.

She moved fast, taking him by the shoulders and pushing him down on to the mattress. She began pulling at his trousers. 'Stop struggling,' she said.

'I've told you it's no good trying to seduce me.'

'If I thought it was, I wouldn't be doing this. And if you want to go to America, you'll start to co-operate. You can get two years' penal servitude just for trying to sell your pass.'

'Mr Snelling won't dare report me.'

She had the waistband of his trousers around his ankles, and was leaning her elbow on his windpipe.

'I will, unless you behave yourself.' She tickled his stomach. He giggled. Angelica looked down and saw he was not as unmoveable to an approach from the opposite sex as he had claimed. She stood up. 'Pull the cover over yourself. You're ill.'

He lay there looking at her pleadingly.

Angelica felt a terrible impulse to join him. It would keep him where he was without protest. He was younger than her, handsome, and a challenge no woman had conquered before. After his conduct in the brothel, what moral right had Worth to protest?

'I've brought your sick note, letting you off work tomorrow.' She spoke more severely than she had intended. 'Now I'm going to give you your medicine.'

She took from her wickerwork bag the flask of clouded

liquid prepared from two of Dr Tang's twists of mushroom powder.

'That's not the sort of medicine I prefer,' said Perugia.

She smiled. 'This is the first dose. In half an hour you'll be much readier for the other.' It was true, though not in the sense she hoped Perugia assumed.

'You're trying to poison me.'

'I've been seen coming here twice. If the police found a corpse, it'd be me they'd come looking for.'

'You could be in England or Germany by then.'

The script had been written and there was no avoiding it. There was a double dose in the flask.

'I take a sip. Now you take one. I take one. Now you. . .'

After five minutes, he said, 'Why don't I feel anything?'

Angelica was beginning to do so. 'Close your eyes and concentrate.'

She put into her bag all Perugia's clothes that she could find.

'How are you feeling?' she asked him.

'Your face has a golden veil in front of it. Why is your neck wobbling so beautifully?'

On the way back to the apartment, Angelica saw the paving stones become bright green and the buildings take on a purple hue. Her body felt weightless. Her inner thighs tingled more and more pleasantly. She loved Worth more passionately than any woman had ever loved a man. She had to struggle with her mind to recall their address.

By the middle of the evening the effect was wearing off. She felt very heavy. She had a slight throbbing in the back of her neck. 'I felt so happy. Where have I been?' she asked. Worth left her to sleep it off and went himself to 13 Rue Ravignon with another dose.

Perugia opened his eyes and saw a man standing over him.

'Did we do wrong? I felt so happy.'

'I am from Venus,' said Worth. 'Drink this, and you can join me there.'

He gave the bottle to Perugia, who drank enough of it to sustain him at least until Monday afternoon.

10

It was after closing time at Maxim's. Through the dawn twilight, a couple could be seen climbing the padlocked wicket-gate into Morin's boat rental yard by the Pont d'Austerlitz. Their laughter could be heard still more easily.

The man, in dinner jacket and black silk trousers, went over first. The woman, in an azure satin Empire gown designed by Gallet, passed him a picnic basket and a portable gramophone. She placed her hands on his shoulders and stepped on to the gate's narrow wooden crossbeam. He clamped his hands on either side of her waist and swung her upwards and towards him.

Her giggles changed into an equally girlish shriek. 'You're tearing my gown. Put me down.'

When her feet were on the ground, she said, 'Can't you wait till we're on the boat?' Her voice was too loud. 'Rip it off me there.'

The watchman was a slow waker. He came to them as they were unhitching a sleek, six-seater rowing punt from its moorings. The picnic basket and the gramophone were already on board. 'What do you think you're doing?'

'Look,' said the woman in the torn dress. 'The working-class has arrived.'

The man in the dinner jacket said, 'We're taking one of your boats.'

The watchman suddenly became more awake. 'The yard's closed, all day Mondays.'

'That's why we're having to steal it.'

The woman giggled again.

'What do you want it for?'

'Isn't it obvious?'

'This is a rowing punt, not a day hotel.'

The woman asked, 'Then why's it supplied with all those cushions? And the striped tent-cover?'

The man asked: 'How much do you want? We're in a hurry.'

The woman raised her skirt almost to knee-level, jumped into the back and tumbled on to the down-filled upholstery. 'My gown's been torn a bit more.'

'Five francs for the hire plus two hundred cash deposit. In case you don't bring it back.'

The man took off his jacket and tossed it into the sharp-pointed bow. That was three times what the boat had cost. 'I'll need your official receipt.'

'A hundred.'

The rowing punt was pushed clear of the dock, and began to float downstream on the Seine's mud-tide. Worth pulled back the striped awning along the centre-strut. What detective reviewing that afternoon the morning's minor incidents within a radius to three kilometers around the Louvre would consider it for more than a moment? Lepine, informed by his own sense of guilt and driven by the infantry-sergeant strutting around his brain, assumed a professional thief to adopt as grave an approach as his.

They had gone to bed early, but had not slept or made love. Angelica pulled her gown over her head, then dropped it over the side into the river. They touched one another and their excitement was fierce. Before they came together again might be a long while, or never. They had almost ten minutes.

The rowing punt bobbed on a sodden wilderness of river weeds, its side knocking against the bank of Ile St Louis. Angelica bundled her hair tightly to the back of her head, and wrapped it in a black muslin scarf. She took a pair of blue dungarees from the picnic basket and began to put them on.

Worth was already dressed and was levering the boat away from the weeds with an oar. He rowed the boat into the current between the island and the right bank, then let it go with the stream while he took Perugia's lunchbox from the basket. He examined his face in the mirror.

Through the awning, the sun was a precisely drawn yellow-red circle. Paris was very quiet. Through the gap in the awning, they saw to their left, over the roof-tops, the twin towers of Notre Dame. Worth steered the punt towards the right bank.

To confirm to himself the certainty of their planning, he did not re-check the contents of his pockets or the box. He refused himself leave to kiss Angelica.

The boat reached the cool stripe of dusk beneath the grimy arch of Pont Neuf. He grasped the lunchbox and jumped to the embankment.

'Stop shifting around,' said the Chief-Ganger, 'and get into line.'

The men in the courtyard shuffled on the cobbles. They wore faded workclothes and peaked caps. Each clutched his lunchbox. In the rollcall of eighty, only twelve names had been struck from the paysheet as absent without permission. Illegal immigrants not only accepted low wages but reported for work.

'You knew enough French to get your jobs. So when I tell you, you'll stand in a *straight* line. *Silently.*'

Worth stood twelfth from the right. The clock in the dome of Gare d'Orsay across the river gave out seven chimes. The Sud Express for Bordeaux and Barcelona was due to leave at 8.12.

'Number off from the right. First eight men, to the photographic studio. You've four minutes to get there.'

A man with only half a left ear tried to catch Worth's eye. 'Goddam,' he said. 'Do a favour for Alwan. I've got a bad ankle. I'll give you a franc to swap.'

Worth pretended not to hear. Later that morning, the studio messengers would become the first suspects.

'What's going on there?' demanded the Chief-Ganger, coming towards them.

'He was trying to swap with me, sir,' said the half-eared man.

'What's your name?'

'Perugia, V.'

'I'm noting it, in case you try that again. You and the rest of your group, to the library.'

Angelica tied the bow of the rowing punt to the iron ring by the outlet of the air tunnel, leaving the stern free to swing round on the current.

She turned the handle of the Dance-All-Night gramophone, winding the coil-spring as tightly as it would go. She slotted the horn into its bayonet socket and put a twelve-inch record on the turntable. She pulled down the automatic-repeat lever.

'*Put my hand in yours, my dear. Clutch me to your breast,*' Mademoiselle Florence Cove sang softly to the accompaniment of the Tottenham Strings. '*Like flowers that bend on the breeze of spring we'll. . .*'

Angelica looked through the gap up on to the towpath. A man walking his dog turned his face away with distaste at what he imagined to be going on beneath the striped cover.

After he reached the corner, she loosened the flap. She stepped on to the backboard, put her arms inside the tunnel and jerked herself upwards. The boat swung out from beneath her feet.

'*Take me in your arms, my dear. Press your lips on mine.*'

After five yards, she was in darkness. The air was warm and sour. She crawled another thirty yards, until the tunnel narrowed and sloped upwards more steeply. She turned on her back and arched it, pushing herself forwards with the rubber heels of her shoes.

Worth put his lunchbox on a half-empty shelf just inside the library door. Foreman Tonnat was rhubarb-faced, brandy-bellied and thin-legged.

'Move that junk from this table,' said Foreman Tonnat, pointing to a pile of books and folios of engravings on the large square reading desk beneath the high window, 'to the next one.'

Two Algerians and an elderly Spaniard gathered them into their arms, walked away and dropped them.

'Now sit down.' Foreman Tonnat was sitting already on the upholstered sedan. 'How many of you have worked under me in here before?'

Five of the eight — the Algerians, the Spaniard, a slim Levantine and a middle-aged Scot — raised their hands.

'Then I'll explain again. I'm a strict foreman. If you're insolent once, I dock you a day's pay. If you're insolent twice, you're sacked on the spot with the week's loss of wages. I'm dividing you into two teams. One will fart around with the books, dusting them and putting them back on the shelves *according to their classifications*. The other will play cards with me. Any questions so far?'

'Sir, we've not been issued with dusters.'

'Use your sleeve.'

The Spaniard asked, 'Can I be look-out man?'

'It's Monday. There's no guard patrol for forty minutes. When we need a look-out, I'll tell you.'

Foreman Tonnat's game was the Mediterranean one of *Méchoula*. There was no draw for banker and dealer; he was both. 'Place your bets, gentlemen.'

The backs of the cards had been marked in Atlanta code. Worth had twenty-five centimes in the pot. He glanced around the other hands, face-down on the table. 'Stick.'

'It's against library rules. Raise and draw or throw in.'

Worth threw in. He dared not look at his watch. According to the library clock, he had seven minutes in which to escape.

In the second round, he raised twice. The others players abandoned their cards, leaving him in lone contest with the bank. Tonnat raised. Worth doubled. The elderly Spaniard shifted uneasily on his chair, and breathed in the heavy odour of impending trouble.

Without a word, Tonnat threw in. Worth cleared four francs sixty — most of it the foreman's.

Dealing the third round, Tonnat raised his eyes from the pack towards Worth, who was staring openly at the backs at his neighbours' cards.

The dealing stopped. Worth glanced inquiringly. 'We've taken a dislike to your face. It puts us off our game. Go and stand watch. You'll hear the guard coming. Shut the door quietly and call to us.'

Worth rose from the table, scooping up his winnings.

The foreman's lips were becoming purple. 'Don't be insolent a second time. Put the money back on the table. We're going to play for you.'

Worth put the money back. 'I raise on high blacks and evens. I always throw in if I'm dealt a red jack.'

The remaining players studied the backs of their hands.

The Salon Carré was four hundred yards away. If Worth left before the sergeant-guard entered, they would meet coming towards one another in a corridor or on the stairs. The sergeant-guard was late.

Worth thought of Angelica, pushing herself backwards up the tunnel; of Louis Lepine, having completed fifty early-morning press-ups, swallowing two raw eggs; of a locomotive shunting the Sud Express's empty passenger carriages from the cleansing shed to Platform Eleven at Gare d'Orsay.

The sergeant-guard's footsteps came down the corridor. From behind him, Worth heard, 'Bank pays black kings.'

Foreman Tonnat sat with his back to the door. Worth did not shut it. Before dealing the next round, Tonnat called, 'Do you hear anything yet, look-out?'

'Nothing yet, sir.'

'That round, you lost three francs. We'll try again for you this time.'

One of the Algerians laughed.

The sergeant-guard came into the library. Worth was moving books from one side shelf to another. The sergeant-guard, looking towards the reading table, went forward quickly.

It would take perhaps five minutes for the *Méchoula* game to be broken up, for the men to be sent to work, for Foreman Tonnat to be reprimanded, and for the money to be confiscated and pocketed.

Worth quietly picked up his lunchbox and left.

Since the guillotining of Louis XVI a hundred and eighteen

years ago, the Louvre had not been used by France's later kings and emperors as a royal palace. But it retained the concealed network of passages and stairs, installed so that servants could move about without affronting regal eyes and nostrils. In the direction from which the sergeant-guard had come, Worth walked down the centre of the broad, mirrored corridor and turned left, into a dark passage.

At the top of the iron spiral staircase, he pushed open the spring-hinged door in the outer panelling, and stepped into the hall of French landscape paintings.

According to the duty roster, it should have been empty. A uniformed concierge sat on a chair, eating a cheese sandwich.

'What are you doing, foreigner?'

'Taking a short cut. To fetch a painting from the north gallery.'

'What's your name?'

Worth chose one from the morning rollcall. 'McDowell, M.'

'Don't stare. Hurry along.'

The Mona Lisa was sixty yards away. The concierge could follow his progress for the first twenty, into the Hall of Martial Triumphs. Walking steadily, without external hesitation, Worth came into the line of vision of the Chief-Ganger, strolling towards him from the other end of the long gallery.

Worth straightened himself, held his head erect and swung his free arm in time with his brisk step. He marched smartly past huge canvases, depicting Napoleon's battlefield victories over the Italians. He came into the Chief-Ganger's focus, who faltered for a moment, then put himself into marching step. Ten yards from the entrance to the Salon Carré, they passed one another, eyes-front and without acknowledgement.

Worth advanced three paces further before the Chief-Ganger halted and turned. 'Where do you think you're going, foreigner?'

'The employees' urinals.'

'What's your name?'

'Abruzzi, G.'

'You're supposed to go in your own time. We're short-staffed. It's not yet half-past seven.'

'To clean them.'

136

The Chief-Ganger looked at him sharply. 'With your hands?'

'He said I'd been disobedient.'

'What's your foreman's name?'

'He didn't tell me.'

'Didn't he make you out a punishment slip?'

'He was angry. Perhaps he suffers from the weather.'

'You're irritating. Follow me.'

By the side door to the vestibule at the entrance to the Salon Carré, he said, 'In the wooden cupboard are rags and ammonia. I'll be back in twenty minutes. If it's not perfect, I'll stand over you while you clean it with your tongue.'

The Chief-Ganger walked on, across the salon. He came level with Mona Lisa and raised his cap to her.

He walked on. Worth was alone.

He kept his eyes from making contact with Mona Lisa's. The alarm was a double-circuit, contact-or-break trigger system. It emerged from the wall behind each side of the picture's frame, looped round the suspension rings and disappeared again into the flock-covered plaster.

He listened, and heard the Chief-Ganger's receding footsteps. He looked round and saw Titian's vast portrayal of calvary looming before him. Three men in a row, nailed to crosses. Two of them for being thieves, the one in the middle for being the Lord from Heaven, for proclaiming the futility of earthly property.

Worth knelt and pulled back the carpet concealing the aligned pressure-pad. He found with his fingers a loose square of parquet which he prised up with his thumbnail.

The cavity beneath was shallow. In it were four pairs of brass screw-fixtures in parallel. Suspended between them were almost hair-thin strands of steel. These had been loosely set, and quivered constantly as though subject to two breezes of equal force coming from opposite directions. They were held apart by a negative current which flowed — via the hooks and the pressure pad — through two small electro-magnets beneath them.

The theory was that a careless hand on one of the picture-hooks or a footfall on the carpet would fracture the fragile porcelain insulation between the supply-lines to the magnets and their auxiliary feeder-wires. The sudden doubling of the wattage would push the steel strands into contact and trigger the alarm in the guardroom. If the supply wires were cut, the sudden loss of current would set off the alarm by causing the strands to spring back against one another.

From his lunchbox, he took his set of postcard reproductions of Louvre paintings and tore them in half lengthways. He ordered his brain to command his heart to slow its rhythm. One. Pause, pause. Two. Pause, pause. Slowly, so as not to create any powerful disturbance of the air in the cavity, he inserted the strips of card between the steel strands, two at a time.

He stood facing Mona Lisa, and returned her smile. He slid the photographic studio docket behind her back, passed its string over the nearest wall-hook, and tied it. He placed the palms of his hands on each side of the frame and repositioned his feet.

As he had practised twice daily since Dr Tang's demonstration, he tightened his shoulder and arm muscles, bent his knees and increased his hand-pressure on the frame until his arms shook in protest. *Ah Choy*!

He tensed his legs. His back muscles felt as though they were about to split.

As Mona Lisa slid upwards, she let out a small, distinct, unnerving shriek. Worth, breathing heavily, saw that it had been caused by friction with the wall-covering. The top of the frame began to swing out towards him from above. He guided it slowly, until Mona Lisa's forehead was touching his, through the glass.

He strengthened his grip on her sides again, and reversed their positions, so he was leaning against the wall, and she against him.

Now for the part Dr Tang had not taught him. A slip, and she would be on the ground with a mighty crash, snapped in two down the fragile grains of the wood on which she had been painted. He forced his elbows downwards, beneath the bottom of the frame. He relaxed his hands on her sides a little, and she slid down until her weight rested on the crook of his arms.

Cradling her thus, he carried her gently to the staff vestibule. He lowered her to the floor, returned to the Salon Carré, and carefully removed the strips of card from the alarm box. He replaced the parquet lid, and pulled back the carpet over it.

Angelica had reached the end of the tunnel, where it connected with the airshaft. Despite the quilted padding next to her skin, her shoulders, elbows and the cheeks of her bottom felt bruised.

In the darkness, she could not tell what time it was. What had gone wrong for Worth? Would she see him again? She strained her head upwards, trying to detect a chink of light or a tiny sound in the shaft above her. There was only the downward rush of foul air. She coughed in its dankness. Would she be lying there if she had been a man and Worth a woman?

Mona Lisa faced the wall, behind the bolted door. Worth, squatting behind her, dripped more linseed oil into the gap between the frame and the fourth and most stubborn of the iron bars still holding her captive.

Again, he inserted the specially shaped corner of his toughened metal comb into the slot of the screw. If it refused to concede to him this time, he would have to use the hacksaw blade in his length of garlic sausage, or break the frame. The frame, made in Sienna by Arbidelli, was more valuable than many of the paintings on display in the museum; but to saw laboriously through the screw could take so long as to risk him missing the train. Before the comb snapped, the screwhead shifted a tenth of an inch. Worth picked the broken piece from the floor with his left hand; his right hand pressed hard down on the iron bar, and it yielded protestingly.

He carefully lifted the heavy wooden block from the frame. As he turned it over, Mona Lisa glowed in the sunlight pouring through the window. Through the cracked surface of dirt, her lips smiled with a knowing fondness; her brilliant eyes were without fear and full of tenderness. This was the woman no foreigner but Morgan had seen, in the company of his crippled, quietly hating and hateful wife. Worth wrapped her in the woollen shawl he had had concealed around his waist beneath his jacket, and lowered her into his lunchbox.

The grille of the air-vent came away easily from the skirting. He unwound the sea-angling rope from around his chest. He slip-knotted it twice around the box. He lowered the box into the shaft. The rope slipped through his fingers rapidly, and then slowed. It went slack, and he felt two tugs. He dropped the end of the rope down and replaced the grille.

Worth unbolted the door between him and the half-empty, almost silent museum. He picked up the frame and glass and carried them down into the servants' staircase. At the bottom he hid them in the darkness beneath the steps. With an ammonia soaked cloth, he wiped the frame clean of his finger-marks. Then he impressed on to its top a single, near-perfect left thumb-print. In front of him was a door leading to the Vincenti court-yard, and beyond that a gate to the street. He snapped off the door handle, forced open the mortice lock with the handle of his comb. He turned, and retraced his footsteps to the library.

'I'm honoured that you've condescended to pay me a visit,' said Foreman Tonnat. 'I've missed your company.'

His bulbous hand flew towards Worth's cheek, to give it a stinging blow. Worth dodged.

'Can't even take your punishment, you cheating sod?'

'No, sir.'

'What've you been up to?'

'When the sergeant-guard arrived, I was worried you'd be cross. I went away for a while until you cooled down.'

The foreman's eyes bulged at him. 'I'll tell you what we'll do. Fine you five francs and dismiss you for the rest of the day without pay. Give this chit to the guard at the gate. Now bugger off before I get angry.'

'Take my hand in yours, dear, and press it to my lips . . .'

Angelica, wearing a grey silk travelling cape, dropped the fishing rope in the river. She released the boat from its line under Pont des Arts, to allow it to drift down to Rouen on the lowering tide. Later that day, someone would report to the police the discovery of an unpeopled rowing punt containing an empty champagne bottle in a picnic basket, a gramophone, a man's shirt and trousers and a set of expensive, hardly-worn female underwear. The *Marie Céleste* had offered no more intriguing a mystery.

She walked quickly to the metro, and rode on it to Austerlitz. At the railway station, she bought a day-return ticket to Gare d'Orsay, and retrieved her wicker dress-case from the left-luggage office, where she had deposited it the afternoon before.

In the tiny embankment garden by the Pont des Arts, Worth found his lunchbox in the midst of the gladioli bush. Inside was a brown paper packet, tied with parcel string. The bicycle was leaning against the tree. It was still padlocked; but three of its spokes had been broken. The frustrated thief had taken defeat badly, slashing the tyres before he left.

Worth had seventeen minutes. He dropped the snapped door handle by the bicycle and stripped off his dungarees. Underneath, he was wearing a dark blue linen suit. He clipped the ready-made bow tie to his collar, picked up the packet, and set off for the station on foot.

As he crossed the bridge, Gare d'Orsay came into view and he began to almost run towards it. It was not considered a crime to be in a hurry to catch a train.

Worth strode into the entrance hall, and up to a porter. 'Take this parcel from me. It's heavy and fragile.'

'What shall I do with it, sir?'

'Hold it without dropping it.'

He went to the ticket window. 'Sud Express. First class sleeping compartment 5G with private bath. To Barcelona. Reserved for Mr Menderes.'

'Hurry, Mr Menderes,' said the clerk, collecting the money and passing over the reservation slip.

'Follow me,' Worth called to the porter.

The brown-liveried conductor saluted Worth when he reached platform eleven, and again when he saw the porter was tipped a ten-franc note.

'It's heavy,' the conductor said.

'And fragile,' Worth said. 'Put it on the rack.'

'Is there anything else you require, sir?'

The sun-blinds had already been lowered. 'Not to be disturbed until we reach Bordeaux. Then whisky and seltzer, smoked sturgeon and loin of veal.'

'No wine, sir?'

'No wine.'

'That'll be eight francs.'

'Don't bring the change,' said Worth, giving him twenty. 'Shut the door behind you.'

The district train from Ivry via Austerlitz steamed into platform twelve two minutes late at 8.06. It was the last train for clerical workers before the offices opened at 8.30.

Another minute, and he raised the sun-blind on the far side of his compartment. An open window of the two-carriage local was less than three feet away. The people on board were in a hurry to get off — all but one. Angelica came across the carriage towards him, releasing the catch on her dress-case.

Beneath the make-up concealing the tunnel-grime, her face was strained. They neither spoke, nor risked the distraction of looking into each other's eyes. She balanced the open case on the window ledge, and he put the parcel inside it.

She snapped the case shut, handed Worth the return portion of her ticket, stepped down on to the platform and hurried to join the crowd filing past the ticket collector.

The guard of the Sud Express blew his whistle. The driver blasted steam through the locomotive's piston outlets. Worth gripped the luggage rack, climbed on to the ledge and slid through the window and into the local.

The Sud Express's couplings engaged with a jolt, and the *train de luxe* began to move forward towards Barcelona, 786 miles away. It clattered across the south-western junction points and accelerated from view around the bend.

The morning studio session at the Louvre would end in a little under four hours. The paintings would be carried back and re-hung in the public galleries. One gap on the wall would remain.

At Bordeaux, at about half-past four in the afternoon, Mr Menderes and his heavy rectangular parcel would be found missing from his compartment of the Sud Express.

By then, Mr Menderes could have alighted at Toury, Orléans, Blois, Tours, Port-de-Piles, Poitiers or Angoulême.

Worth left the local at Austerlitz, handed in the return portion of the ticket and took a taxi to the apartment.

Angelica's dress-case was on the bed. He took out the parcel and unwrapped the painting. He carried it to the servants' wash-room, which he had converted into a photographic dark-room. He placed it, face up, on the folded layers of Belgian linen in the rectangular ceramic tray on the bench beneath the enlarger, whose bulb glowed dimly through the colour-filter.

In the thin red light amid the matt-black walls, Mona Lisa's eyes became recessed and sullen. Her smile was more pronounced and tinged with defiance.

The chemist's thermometer in the pot on the spirit stove registered 112 degrees. He dipped the velour brush into the viscous, molten solution, and began to coat her with the first layer of pharmaceutical gelatin.

11

'Where have I been? What happened to me?' Perugia lay on his back on his bed, exhausted by Dr Tang's hallucinatory voyage. 'This is the worst hangover I've ever had, worse than meths.'

His unshaven cheeks were hollower than before. Dark rings were round his eyes which he was trying to fix on Angelica, but which kept dropping towards their lower lids.

'Stay lying there, very calmly.' She spoke in a nursing sister's voice, gave him a nursing sister's alarmist smile. 'You've done something important. You've stolen the Mona Lisa from the Louvre.'

He neither moved his limbs nor blinked while he tried to search his mind. 'That's rubbish.' He spoke slowly. 'Nobody steals the Mona Lisa from the Louvre.'

'Just stay calm.' Surely the irritating commands must soon jolt him in the opposite direction. 'Read this.'

His hand reached out uncertainly, and took from her the special edition of *Le Temps*.

'Mona Lisa Reported Stolen.' He mumbled the words aloud. 'The Mona Lisa has been reported stolen. The acting curator of the Louvre reported its theft to the Prefect, Mr L. Lepine, shortly after midday.

'The office of the Prime Minister, Mr Caillaux, announced that he is returning to Paris from his country residence, together with other ministers, and will preside over an emergency cabinet meeting early this evening.'

Perugia paused. 'It doesn't say I stole it.'

'Where's it say you didn't?'

Perugia leant on his elbow. 'Mr Lepine, appealing for public calm, said that the thief was almost certainly identified and

that the painting would quickly be restored in perfect condition to the Louvre, perhaps within twenty-four hours.

'Large crowds around the museum obstructed the arrival of
police, to search the premises and question employees.'

'If I did it, how do you know?'

'After you went to work this morning, you had an argument
with the foreman. After a second warning, he dismissed you
for the day for insolence and docked your pay. You left the
Louvre via the Salon Carré. After you'd gone, the painting was
found missing. You took it out in your lunchbox.'

'I couldn't have done. It would have been searched by the
guard at the gate.'

'Look around you. Your lunchbox is missing. It's been
found on the embankment below the museum.'

'Are you from the police?'

'I'm trying to protect you from them. In a few hours, they'll
be round here to check on you. They'll take your left thumb-
print. Don't leave this room until they have. Move around,
make sure you're seen through the window. They've no way of
knowing the lunchbox is yours. I've brought you another you
can show them. All you're to tell them is you had a row with
the foreman, and he sent you home.'

'But why did I do it?'

'You thought you were Leonardo da Vinci's reincarnation,
and that the painting was yours.'

'Where have I hidden it?'

'If you can't remember, the better you'll stand up to police
questioning.'

Perugia had become steadier. He looked at her earnestly,
bleakly and without hatred. 'Mr Snelling's sent you, to frame
me.'

He sat up, as though to get dressed. He looked at the empty
chair, at the floor beside the bed. He wrapped a sheet around
himself and went to the cupboard. 'I've brought your clothes
back from the laundry in this basket. Where do you want to
go?'

'You're paying me the money. I'm catching the train to
Genoa. Then I'm buying two steamship passages to America.

Mr Snelling and the police and the rest of you'll never find me again.' He sniffed phlegm back from his nostrils to his throat and swallowed. 'There's a lot of painters in New York, and they don't welsh on their own.'

'The police are searching the international trains, watching the sea-ports.'

Perugia withdrew from the cupboard, pulling out his scuffed and slightly warped canvas-covered cabin-trunk. 'Just give me the money. I'll never tell on you.'

'They're looking and watching for Louvre employees. From the moment the police come here and find you've gone, it'll be you they're hunting — probably only you. They'll send you to Devil's Island.'

'They couldn't prove it. After a row with the foreman, I've the right to leave and go home to Italy.'

'You've lost your intelligence again as fast as it came back. France has lost the Mona Lisa. The most valuable object that exists. When the French arrest you, if you tell them where you've hidden it, and they find it there undamaged, they might let you go after ten or twenty years. Until you do, they won't.'

Perugia sat on the cabin-trunk. 'I'd tell them everything I know. Mr Snelling, the other man, you, this conversation. Second, the police can't put me away. A court has to do that.'

'Mr Snelling has been confined to a lunatic asylum throughout. The police would find that the other man doesn't exist, any more than I do. Right now, France's self-respect is looking for a quick conviction of a foreigner. They'll wait for the return of the Mona Lisa until you decide to exchange it for a pardon.'

He was picking at the nail of his big toe. 'Even I don't know I did it. I'm innocent until proved guilty. There are defence lawyers.'

'If you could afford one, he'd wear black robes and represent you from the pit of the court. The prosecutor wears scarlet silk and stands on the dais with the judges. The jury will be all French. When they retire, the presiding judge will go in with them and guide them. I'm trying to protect you.'

'You bastards,' said Perugia, with the defeatist resentment

nurtured by long residence in L'Enclave. 'What do you want me to do?'

'Mr Snelling will get you to New York. If you don't want to spend the rest of your life in jail instead, put your trunk back in the cupboard, go back to bed and stay there until the police come.'

'Then give me some medicine.'

'It's not good for you any more.'

The final batch of employees was allowed to leave the Louvre soon after six in the evening, their initial interrogations completed, their prima facie innocence — if not their lack of complicity — confirmed by the whorled contours of their left thumb-tips. Five who had been dismissed for the day, before the theft was discovered, had been checked in their homes by members of the fingerprint squad, and had also been cleared.

That had been the only new news in the statement read to reporters in the museum's main lobby by Inspector Charon, the Prefecture's spokesman. During the remainder of the tense, brief press conference, Lepine stood silently by Charon's side, as the questions became longer and the replies more terse.

Had the Prefecture identified a suspect?

Yes, and no.

More than one?

No comment.

Could Inspector Charon state whether or not the theft was a German provocation, designed to humiliate France?

That was a question for the German Ambassador.

Given the Government's pledge to abolish administrative ineptitude and the fact that the theft could have taken place implied bungling of a major order, was a political motive suspected?

The inspector was not a politician.

When would an arrest be made?

When the thief and the painting were captured.

Lepine's eyes roamed through the pack of perspiring journalists. Worth nodded, trying to catch his attention. Lepine turned and walked away.

Outside, gendarmes were digging through the flower beds, and two were being lowered on a rope down an open sewer manhole. On the other side of the temporary barrier which had been erected, spectators watched them through rented binoculars. The shocked *gravitas* with which the painting's disappearance was being treated impressed Worth beyond his expectations. Almost two hundred detectives and more than a thousand uniformed police had been drafted into the Louvre. Dujardin-Beaumetz, the Minister for Art, had sent a telegram of dismissal to Dr Homolle, the museum's director holidaying in Greece. Then the Prime Minister had sacked Dujardin-Beaumetz. The cabinet was still meeting. The National Assembly had been recalled from its summer recess three weeks early. Tomorrow, there was to be an emergency session to debate a motion of no confidence. Deputies were unlikely to be appeased by Dujardin-Beaumetz's political slaughter; the Government would have to lobby through the night to survive.

A policeman unlocked the Manège gate to allow Worth into the street. A crowd, four and more deep, was peering through the railings. A pedlar offered a hurriedly-framed sketch of the section of wall from which the Mona Lisa was missing. Worth bought it.

'There's one of them,' said an old woman.

'I heard him too,' said a one-armed man. 'Talking with a German accent.'

Worth sprinted across the street into the Café des Académiciens, and left through the side exit before his pursuers had reached the front door.

The apartment's doorbell rang just before nine in the morning. Mona Lisa was glowering in the darkroom beneath a further coating of pharmaceutical gelatin. Worth and Angelica were in bed, drinking black coffee, checking the text of his press cablegram for New York to ensure it contained nothing which had not been published in the Paris newspapers.

Worth, in dressing gown, opened the front door. Snelling stood in the hall.

'It's all right,' he said quietly. 'I won't try to come in.'

His spell in the insane asylum had transformed him. He had lost perhaps fifteen pounds of beer belly. His face was no longer flushed, and his complexion had cleared. He was wearing a brand-new, off-the-peg suit and seemed markedly composed.

'How did you escape?'

'They let me out this morning. They gave me these clothes and said I was on probationary leave, free to go anywhere I wanted in Paris.'

'Mr Snelling, I don't have your notebook.'

Snelling smiled with remorse. 'I realise now. I must have dropped it on the floor of the restaurant washroom. I'm afraid I acted over-angrily afterwards. But I'm cured of that now.' There was no hint of irony in his subdued voice. 'Thanks to you.'

'How did you find me?'

'I asked for your address, and they wrote it down.'

'Mr Snelling, I'm gratified that you should come to repay me, but give it no more thought. I hold myself in part to blame for the episode.'

Snelling swallowed, for the first time displaying a little nervousness. 'Can you consider . . .' He paused. 'Sir, I have some urgent business it's important they shouldn't know about yet. Please can you advance another hundred francs on top of what I owe? You have my word as a Pinkerton man you'll be repaid.'

Worth did not conceal his surprise. 'Are you sure you're still a Pinkerton man?'

'I will be again, soon, if you'll give me the money I need now.'

'Mr Snelling, you've had troubles enough in this city.' Worth put a firm hand on his shoulder. 'Take a boat home.'

'Sir, if I did, I could never face myself or Larreen again. I beg you.'

On his return journey to the front door with ten ten-franc notes in hand, Worth passed by the window, and saw the plain-clothes man at the corner.

After he gave Snelling the money, he said, 'Someone's following you.'

'He won't be for long.' Snelling turned and began to step briskly down the stairs.

Had Lepine freed a cat to stalk the rat? He went into the darkroom. The new coating of gelatin had set. Through its brown mist, Mona Lisa stared at him resentfully. He brushed on the third layer.

In the name of the Republic of France, I take oath and charge before the Court of Investigation that on or about August 22, 1911, a painting, reputed to be a portrayal of Madonna Lisa della Gherardini executed by Master Leonardo da Vinci, legal property of the Republic, was unlawfully removed from its proper place in the Louvre Palace, Paris, 1st District, without intention to return it, by Mr X, subsequently to be identified to the Court.

Master of Law L.M. Lescouves,
State Prosecutor.

The Spanish prisoner, Pablo Ruiz Picasso, painter, aged 30 years, burst into tears. He had been arrested at two o'clock that morning, and most of the time since had been questioned, first by police and then by Master Lescouves.

The Louvre remained closed to the public. The Court of Investigation was taking its hearings in the library, where Worth had been dismissed four days before. The book-stacks had been pushed back on their gantries to make space for the press and distinguished visitors. Worth was lodged on the edge of the bench in the fourth row, which had been grudgingly allocated — after protests from the Anglo-American Press Association — to foreign news agencies.

'Give the prisoner your handkerchief, Master Lescouves,' the judge ordered. 'And let the Court be cleared of journalists.'

Judge Drioux sat behind the square reading table, in the chair more usually occupied by Foreman Tonnat. The case had been evaded by the stipendiaries at the Palace of Justice. Drioux's career had been in the colonial magistracy in Indo-

China. Now seventy-six, he had been called from his retirement in Hyeres.

Defence lawyer Pétain, retained by the state to represent the still-unnamed defendant, rose from a librarian's stool. 'On behalf of Mr X, I protest. He has the right under Article 192 for the Press to be present at all times.'

The judge referred to his red-covered manual of procedure. 'Then the Press may remain. But there is nothing in 192 entitling them to take notes or report if I say not, and I do. Master Pétain, is the prisoner before me your client?'

'Your honour, that is for the Court to say.'

'Your honour,' Master Lescouves intervened. 'The name "Mr X" is a technical device, to avoid judicial delay in an exceptionally serious and urgent criminal case such as this. The Court of Investigation cannot begin hearings until a charge is laid against a person, even if the identity is unknown.'

Judge Drioux reached for his water-glass with a trembling hand. 'While you were attending a convent infant school, I was teaching French law to savages.'

He turned to Master Pétain. 'Do you agree with this summary of this morning's evidence? Mr Picasso is an artist. His friend, Mr Apollinaire, is an art critic and admirer of his work. On Mr Picasso's thirtieth birthday, Mr Apollinaire gave him a small stone carving, which he himself had received previously as a gift from a lady-friend, Olivia, who herself had been given it by Guy Pieret, who was then employed as an inventory-clerk in the Louvre's storerooms.'

Judge Drioux lowered his head towards his notes. 'Olivia has since had an argument with Mr Pieret. She recalls his parting words as, "Next time you want something from the Louvre, find someone else to get it." A door was slammed. It's said, and I don't believe this, that the reference was assumed at the time to be to *Les Magasins du Louvre*, the department store.'

Judge Drioux sipped water. 'Mr Apollinaire, learning of the theft of the Mona Lisa, referred to the Louvre's catalogue and found in one an illustration of the stone carving in question. He went to Mr Picasso and confessed.

'Both these men are foreigners without the right of permanent residence in France. They feared it was Pieret who'd stolen the Mona Lisa, that he'd be arrested and would inform on them as receivers of goods stolen from the Louvre.

'So they bought him a one-way rail ticket to Berlin, got him drunk and bundled him on board the train. They put the stolen carving into a shopping bag and set out last night to dump it in the River Seine. They found its banks swarming with police, panicked and were arrested.'

Judge Drioux shuddered. 'Gentlemen, this Court hasn't been convened to inquire into a carving, the residential status of foreigners or Mr Picasso's weird talents. I am here, without pleasure, to confirm the identity of the thief of the Mona Lisa.'

Through the open window above the judge's head came sounds of cheering. The museum had become a still greater summer attraction than it had been when open. On the other side of the wall, visitors to Paris lined the museum's south promenade, watching police in rowing boats drag-netting the Seine, and sarcastically applauding each time an object was pulled up to the surface — a rusted bicycle, a broken paving stone, the weighted carcass of a dog.

'I call Prefect Lepine. We are still *in camera*.'

The judge gazed without fondness at the great detective, and did not invite him to sit. 'I have been here almost a week, waiting for you to bring me Mr X. You have made fifteen arrests, not one of which has been of the man you are supposed to be looking for.'

Lepine interrupted. 'My Department has done so, not myself personally. I have been preoccupied applying my own approach to the case.'

'And what has been established?' The judge blew his nose. 'That the Mona Lisa is no longer in this museum. But there are no means by which it could have been removed undetected. None of the employees present in the museum at the time committed the theft. Nor did the thief enter posing as an employee, as all arrivals and departures through the staff entrance were tallied and have been fully accounted for. All other entrances and exits remained closed throughout. They had not been forced. Neither their locks nor their alarm systems had been tampered with. No windows had been broken through. Neither the sewers nor the air-ventilating conduits are large enough to enable a thief to gain entry or make his escape. Are you suggesting, perhaps, that the theft has been committed by a ghost?'

The judge paused. Lepine seemed about to reply but to change his mind.

'Mr Lepine. This Court, the people of France, and lovers of art all around the world are impatient. You have been blessed with a wealth of forensic evidence to guide your searches. A thumb-print. A handle broken from an internal door, and found abandoned on the embankment together with a lunch-box and a stolen bicycle. A man hurrying to Gare d'Orsay with a heavy parcel, catching the train to Barcelona. Why are these leads not being followed?'

'I am unconvinced of their relevance,' Lepine replied. 'The case presents unusual difficulties.'

The judge sighed, and thought for several seconds. 'Mr Lepine, your reputation has been of the highest. It has been based on brilliantly demonstrating that whatever happens in other countries, there can be in France no such aberration as the committing of a "perfect" major crime. I begin to fear your arrogance. You have been using this Court, and the reporters present, to provide a diversionary spectacle, to distract public attention from your continuing failure to find Mr X.'

Judge Drioux placed his pen in the inkwell. 'This Court adjourns until you assure me you have something sensible to say to it.'

I beg your pardon [Louis Lepine had written] *for having lacked opportunity for a confidential discussion with you until now. My chauffeur will fetch you at six o'clock tonight. Please bring with you a billiards cue.*

The chauffeur did not drive off towards Lepine's residence, but headed north-east.

Worth asked, 'Where are you going?'

'To meet with the Prefect.'

In the ninth district, the Renault Straight-Eight drew to a halt in Rue du Delta, outside a squat yellow stucco building with a façade of mock-Egyptian plaster pillars. Its signboard said:

'TEMPLE OF THE NILOTIC SPIRIT'

Minister: Madame A. Casochok

The chauffeur opened the car door for Worth and took the leather-topped cue, bought in Au Printemps that afternoon, from his hand. 'The Prefect's in the back row, left-hand side.'

The hall was lit dimly with blue-lensed oil lamps. Rows of pews faced a low platform on which a man and a woman sat facing each other on bentwood chairs.

'You'll find this interesting,' Lepine whispered, as Worth sat beside him. 'She's unusual.'

'Silence,' said the man on the platform. 'We must have total silence.'

Someone in the congregation several rows ahead began to cough bronchially.

'If you can't be quiet, make your donation and leave.'

The woman on the platform was in her late sixties at least. She wore a black décolleté gown with a black shawl over her shoulders, in the Mona Lisa style, which had just become fashionable. She sat at a ten degree angle to the hall, striking a Mona Lisa pose, her right hand limply resting on her left wrist. At one second intervals, between drawing in and releasing breath, she quietly said, *'Halom.'*

Worth took out his note-pad, and scribbled, *'Is she saying that's Mr X's name?'*

He handed the pad and pencil to Lepine, who wrote back, *'It's an old Egyptian conjuration. Have patience. She has been doing this every evening since it was stolen.'*

Lepine's mind was faltering, particularly for the religious man he claimed to be. He was hunting ghosts, as Judge Drioux had said.

'Who are you?' the man on the platform asked.

The woman replied, 'Anna.'

'Not Anna. Lisa.'

The woman repeated her spell more slowly, with pauses of

almost two seconds. Her left shoulder dropped, and her torso began to tilt towards the audience. The man did not move forward to help her. Suddenly, as though electrodes had been applied to her feet, she trembled and straightened.

'Lisa!'

She bent the corners of her lips upwards, and spoke in a higher pitch. 'I listen, master.'

'Lisa, where are you?'

'Here. I am here.'

'In Paris?'

'Yes.'

'Where?'

'He has put me in the dark. So dark I cannot see.'

'Can you hear?'

'Yes.'

'Can you hear if he is alone with you? Are there others?'

'I hear a woman too.'

'What do they say?'

'It's a language strange to me.'

'Lisa, what are their names?'

She slumped forward and put her hand to her forehead. 'Who is Lisa?' Her voice was gruff and weak. 'I am Anna.'

'Brilliant,' Lepine said, rising from the pew. 'Remarkable.'

By the sham standards of the fairground seances of Worth's youth, it had been a three-dollar bill performance.

'For such a highly reputed journalist, I'm disappointed by your reaction. You have to look beyond the obvious fact that she's a fraud.' The windowless, wood-panelled snooker room of Lepine's official residence was brilliantly lit with electric lamps. He had dismissed the servants for the evening. A cold buffet had been laid on the sidetable, together with an ice-bucket containing a bottle of Vichy water. 'Like all good fake mediums, she has genuine perception. Astute of her to see the thief as a foreigner. Heads or tails?'

'Heads. It's hardly impressive when she couldn't give his nationality.'

Worth won the toss, and positioned the white ivory ball on

the upper left of the table. Lepine's interest in him was beyond that of gaining newspaper publicity. But why?

As he was taking aim, Lepine said, 'Anna Casochok's been of service to me before. Before tomorrow's seance, I'll let her know he's American.'

Worth aimed again. He struck the white ball hard with his cue, driving it fast across the grass-green baize, between the yellow and the brown. Two-thirds of its way down the table, it bounced off the cushion and pushed its way into the midst of the cluster of reds. 'Why did you arrest nine Frenchmen, two Germans, a Russian, a Spaniard, and no Americans?'

Lepine sharply spun the ball, and potted a red. 'When you lose the toss, the best response is to strike out in an almost random direction.'

He went to the scoreboard on the wall and notched himself a point. He returned to the table, sank the pink, another red, the green, another red. 'Once you start to clear the table, even a little, you begin to see the pattern of the game.'

With his cue, he measured the angle between the white, the brown and the centre pocket. He took a screw shot. The brown missed the hole and bounced back. 'Your break. My thief — and I think of him as mine already — does not merely relish celebrity. He has a refined sense of theatre, which is too self-controlled to be that of a European, other than a Prussian, and yet too inexplicit to be of Germanic inspiration. Forcing one of the few locked doors in the museum he could not have used to make his exit. The "clues" left in the embankment garden. He rushes to the railway station, invites a porter and a conductor to hold his heavy, rectangular parcel. He boards the express bound for Spain, and then dematerialises. Who but a man who'd in his youth admired Harry Houdini's techniques would downstage him like that?'

Worth potted red, brown, red, green, red, yellow, red, pink and then, momentarily distracted, sank the black.

'Penalty,' said Lepine, notching down Worth's score and putting the black back on the table. 'I think you're not new to this game. You forgot how much mental concentration, as well as physical dexterity, even a friendly contest requires.'

A gentleman would have forewarned his opponent if he'd seen him about to make such an error. He had watched silently while Worth planned and executed his. Lepine selected another cue from his rack. 'Then there's the motive. My thief is not insane, though he might soon come to fear he's become so.'

Red. Brown. Red. 'A European would have stolen it for either of two reasons. As a practical joke, probably of a political nature and against the State. To make his point, he would by now have returned the painting, or produced evidence he had it with a threat to destroy it.'

Red. Pink. Red. Green. Red. 'That's got rid of the reds. Or he would have stolen the Mona Lisa to sell on the art black market. None of the dealers have been approached. I had a couple of them in the Prefecture for the night. I offered them and the rest five years immunity from all outstanding prosecutions, for a lead. Nothing.'

Worth said, 'According to your own theory, it's already in the USA, in the hands of a millionaire.'

'Four have put out indiscreet feelers. One is on his way here to try his hand at out-manoeuvring and out-bidding the Government for it. It's a side issue.'

He bent down to table level, and studied the line of sight between the white and the black. He rejected the shot and raised himself again. 'You see, my thief's still in Paris, with the painting. He's waiting as patiently as he's able for the uproar to fade, for France to resign herself to the loss, for the search to be abandoned. Even though he knows that by then, so long will have passed that it will be virtually impossible to authenticate it as the one that was stolen from the Louvre.'

'Why?'

'A painting of that antiquity doesn't remain stable like a bar of gold or a cut diamond or even a sculpture. It changes— how rapidly and how much depends on the atmospheric conditions in which it's stored. Even in ideal ones, it's volatile. The image is composed of differently coloured powders suspended in an emulsion of oil and water which, however perfectly blended, have a natural tendency slowly to separate. Wherever she is, however well she's cared for, the Mona Lisa would not be as she was when last seen in the Louvre.'

'Why is your thief doing this?'

Lepine moved to the far side of the table, aimed at the yellow and missed by almost an inch. His hand on the cue was trembling. 'I don't yet know why. His motives are unusual. I look forward to exploring them with him. What he's trying to do. Make his fortune, obviously, if he hasn't done so already. More disturbing, he's trying to make an ass of me.'

Worth potted the yellow, and took the green. 'It's an extraordinary ambition to attribute to the thief of the century.'

'I hope you're right that he'll prove the last of his calibre. But the century's young. The key to understanding him is that tauntingly near-perfect impression of his left thumb-print on top of the frame.'

Worth sank brown. 'It's not for a guest to suggest his host to be egocentric. But if your thief craves celebrity and will be in need of authentification, leaving his mark hardly constitutes a personal assault on you.'

'Why a thumb-print, when he has so many other means? Because I'm known to disdain fellow detectives who rely on them as evidence. And why his left thumb?'

'It's well-documented that Leonardo painted the Mona Lisa with his left hand.'

'Not with his thumb. Why not leave the impression of one or more of his fingers from the same hand? Because in the print library we have to have at the Prefecture, despite my personal views, and in Scotland Yard or the FBI, all the impressions filed are those of suspects' and criminals' right thumbs. Somewhere, his must be among them.'

Apart from the white, only the black ball remained on the table. The angle was impossible. Worth played a defensive shot, leaving white resting on the cushion. 'Why didn't you tell Judge Drioux this morning?'

'From what you call my egocentricity. I'd have been laughed out of the Court, and so scored a major point against myself, for the thief.'

'When's he going to reveal to the world it's a plot against you?'

'He never will. I'll catch him first, and in the process strangle international theft in its infancy. It's a simple challenge. Either he makes history, or I do. We can't both do so. Those are his terms, not mine. I accept them.' Almost languidly, he pushed the white ball from the cushion back into play against the black. 'I feel his presence in Paris, watching me as closely as he can. He's waiting for me to take an initiative.'

'When will you?'

'Not necessarily when I'm ready. When he is. Have you ever attended a bullfight?'

'They're not to my taste.'

'You should do so soon. In France, it's against our laws and our national character to kill the bull, unless he runs from the ring back to the illusory safety of his pen. The gate is always left open. If he does, he's shot in the head and carted to the butcher's block to be divided and sold off in portions. The matador loses face, his reputation, perhaps his self-respect. What a French crowd expects of him is to fascinate, to hypnotise his bull into wanting to remain in the ring— to make false passes at him, to pierce his hide with darts and daggers. Not to cause him pain, though it obviously does, but to anger him into believing he can kill the matador, into trying to do so until he collapses, exhausted, to be carried off on a stretcher.'

It was Lepine's turn to play again. It needed only a sidespin of the white to sink the black; but he seemed to have forgotten the snooker. 'Come with me to the Prefecture. I think you'll be interested.'

The interrogation cell was about twelve feet square. It had a bare concrete floor. The walls and ceiling had been painted dark green. It contained a bench, an upright chair, a table upon which rested a black-covered Holy Bible, a packet of cigarettes and a glass of brandy. In one corner was a chamber pot. A Hughes microphone, fixed high on the wall above arm's reach was wired to a speaker in the adjoining room, in which Lepine and Worth stood.

Lepine had turned off the light, so that Worth could see more clearly through the small rectangle of glass-covered grillwork into the cell. It took him a few moments to identify the man sitting slumped on the bench as Snelling. His condition was a shocking one, and his low, spasmodic moans could be heard through the speaker. His new jacket had been ripped through to its lining. On his forehead, above his right eye, there was a dark, blood-filling swelling. A two-inch gash on his left cheek had been painted with iodine. His left eye was covered by a ragged white patch with a bright new red stain.

Worth swallowed hard. When he spoke, he did not filter the anger from his voice. 'What'd he do, Mr Lepine? Ask to see his lawyer? Answer a question too slowly? Mutilate himself with the sharp edge of the Bible?'

Lepine replied equably, 'He looked much worse when we brought him in. Almost none of that happened here. I had him released from the asylum, to see where he'd go. When he left you, he tried to throw off our tail at Pigalle metro station. He's still alive because he failed. He walked into L'Enclave and was beaten up. Some illegals have become extra wary since the painting was stolen. They thought him to be a detective. As you can see, they aim for the eyes first.'

'What's his explanation?'

'He won't give one. He demands the US Consul. We've explained to him the consular treaty between our countries specifically excludes certified lunatics. We won't de-certify him until he talks. He won't talk until we de-certify him. This mutually detrimental impasse is now perhaps to be broken by your reunion with him.'

The tone implied the price of hesitation to be an interrogation cell for Worth himself. Coldness, a recurrence of fever. 'What do you want from him?'

'Whatever he has to say to you. The relationship between the two of you does not seem to have been conventional.'

The door of the cell closed behind Worth, and was locked from the corridor side. Snelling recognised him and tried to rise to greet him, but dropped back on the bench with a grunt. 'I'm sorry to see they've brought you in here too, after you did so much for me. I seem to be causing you a lot of trouble.'

'I've been called in to help you.'

Snelling half-straightened himself. 'We must be careful what we say.'

He spoke with the assumption of complicity Worth most feared. 'They're listening through that microphone.'

Worth carried the chair to the wall and climbed on to it. He pulled the wire and stepped down to the concrete. He hoped he had made sufficient noise to cover the sound of the small glass panel being opened by Lepine. 'Are you in pain?'

Snelling nodded. 'Nerves too.'

'Take some brandy and have a cigarette.'

'I've sworn never to touch liquor again. Do you have a cigar?'

Worth selected from his silver pocket-case an Upmann *petit corona*, bit off the end and lit it. 'If you want to get out of this, you must talk frankly.'

'If I do, will you tell them?'

'If it's in your interests. Who were you looking for in L'Enclave?'

Snelling took the cigar and puffed at it rapidly. When the tip glowed and crackled, he inhaled deeply and began to splutter. A large tear dropped out from beneath his eye-patch. He bent forward clutching his ribs. 'Brandy!'

'An oath's an oath. If you need it, pick up the glass yourself.'

Snelling remained where he was. 'I don't remember his name.'

That was a major blessing. 'I strongly advise you to.'

Snelling peered at him through his uncovered right eye. 'Are you working for them?'

'I couldn't be, as an American. I'm trying to get a fellow citizen out of trouble. They think you're involved in the Mona Lisa.'

'I was in hospital. Wish I'd been kept there.'

'Where does he live?'

'The address is in my notebook, underneath his name.'

'Where's the notebook?'

'I dropped it in the toilet the day I was committed.'

'Could you take them to where he lives?'

'I never went there. That's how I got lost in L'Enclave.'

'Would you recognise him if you were shown him again?'

'Obviously. I'm a professional detective.'

The glass panel was ajar and there was no going back. 'Why were you looking for him?'

The cigar dropped from Snelling's fingers to the concrete floor. 'If I'd the choice, I'd rather be convicted of stealing the Mona Lisa. When I was drunk, soon after he came to Paris, I went to a nightclub called *Il est Elle*, and got talking to him. Afterwards we committed an illegal act of indecency. Then he tried to blackmail me into paying for him to emigrate to New York to become a portrait painter. Given the trouble I got into since, I was looking for him to pay him off. If I don't, I'll lose my job and my wife. That's why I came to borrow money from you.'

Worth watched with astonishment as Snelling buried his face in his hands and sobbed, and felt deep professional admiration. Though only to save himself, he had lied impeccably.

'What will you do with him?' Worth sat in an embroidered armchair in Lepine's large corner office, five floors above the interrogation cells in the basement.

The Prefect, as though from habit, stood at the window, looking at the head-lamps of the vehicles crossing Pont Henri IV. 'I'll apologise to him. I was born without sexual inclinations of any variety, but I've little sympathy with the present indecency laws. If it weren't for my interventions, there are exemplary husbands and fathers, several of them in high positions, who'd have been disgraced. Obviously, when it's between two women, one cannot risk such tolerance.'

'Snelling?'

'I can't set him free for fear he'll run towards another catastrophe. For a detective, he is undoubtedly accident-prone. In his present condition, I can't pass him to your consul. I'll have him sent to our refuge in the country, fed well, weaned back on to liquor. Once he's himself, I'll have him deported. Foreign private detective agencies are forbidden by decree from operating in France.'

'You're not going to try to find the blackmailer?'

'When Snelling begins to recover, we'll send down a staff artist to sketch a likeness from his description, and then pick up the little weasel at our leisure.'

'Why did you suspect Snelling?'

Lepine walked to his desk and sat on it. He was suddenly less relaxed and more composed. 'You Americans are puzzling. Today, he greeted you like a long-lost friend. Two weeks ago, he commissioned a psychopath to murder you.'

'I was working on an exposé of Pinkerton's activities in Europe. He came to believe I'd stolen his notebook. I had. He'd written it in code. After Mr Coucelles' visit, I destroyed it, untranscribed. The doctor in your asylum persuaded him he was suffering from a persecutory delusion.'

Lepine leant forward. 'But what was the Pinkerton activity you were exposing? Why did the two of you come to meet in the Louvre, in front of the Mona Lisa?'

'I've a personal grudge against Pinkertons. They cracked my father's skull in a strike bust in ninety-three. After I came to Paris, I saw him in the street. I could recognise him from Worth's funeral in London. I went after him.'

'Do you think he is implicated in the theft?'

'If your American-Millionaire Theory is correct, yes. He would have been sent here to track the thief for the sponsor. He had more than a casual friendship with Coucelles.'

Lepine leant backwards, slowly shaking his head. 'Since the theft, I've become prone to persecutory delusions myself. In my mind, I've seen William Pinkerton as a puppet-master. That we disagree profoundly over techniques of detection is the minor point. I've effectively blocked his agency's expansion into Europe, his dream of taking criminal detection out of public control, into that of a worldwide corporation owned by himself. I even have evidence he did a deal with Worth over the Duchess of Devonshire portrait, while my colleagues at Scotland Yard drank their gin and looked the other way. If he discredits me over the Mona Lisa, he's won. I thought you might be able to guide me, however little or unintentionally, towards Pinkerton as the enemy. Instead, you've steered me towards a shaking sodomite.'

Lepine stood and returned to the window. 'It's a dark world, and becoming darker. I hope we'll be able to resume our snooker match.'

Rewards offered by newspapers for information leading to the Mona Lisa's safe recovery mounted daily, and were distracting the French from their war fever, turning them into a nation of amateur detectives. *Paris Soir* promised ten thousand francs, its rival *La Dépêche* a hundred thousand and *Le Matin* five thousand a year for life. The weekly *La Vie Moderne* offered the stallion which had won the *Grand Prix* at Longchamps, *Progrès* a stateroom on board the first Atlantic voyage of an airship.

For foreign visitors with heavy luggage, citizens' arrests were a new hazard of travel in France. Some Germans, as the nationality under most suspicion, cut short their holidays only to be beaten by vigilantes at the Saar border crossing. The painting itself was spotted in Perpignan, Dijon, Menton, Aix-en-Provence, Lyons and a dozen other places. Frenchmen abroad reported sightings from Dover, Glasgow, Madrid, Istanbul, St Petersburg and Alkmaar.

'Though it's patriotically most commendable, it's seriously hampering our investigations,' said Inspector Charon at the morning press briefing at the Prefecture. 'I beg your editors to offer no more rewards. Even before the theft, there were many times more copies of the Mona Lisa in existence than of any other painting. Quite a few are old— as much as three hundred years old— and can appear to the ignorant to be the original.'

He pointed to a pile of twenty or so Mona Lisas on the table in front of him. 'This morning's submissions. Your readers are buying them in junk shops, taking them from churches, schools, provincial art galleries and other people's houses. They take them to your newspaper offices, and you send the paintings on to us. Every time one arrives, a detective has to stop what he's doing, enter its details on a form three pages long, show it to an expert and obtain from him a written assessment, then try to establish whether it's been stolen and, if it has, arrange its return. We require your co-operation to change the procedure.'

He reached behind him and tugged at a cloth pinned to the wall, revealing an unframed Mona Lisa. Its quality was remarkable — to Worth, in the front row, momentarily disturbing.

'For thirty-seven years, Professor Dr Enrico Bellini has been in sole charge of the restoration work the Mona Lisa needs at regular intervals, to preserve her radiant beauty for posterity. His intimate knowledge of the painting is unsurpassed. He is now eighty-one years old and feels too frail to travel from Italy. When we recover the original, it will be taken to him in Florence for its ultimate verification before being returned to the Louvre.

'Meanwhile, he has sent this replica, which he painted himself. It's more than just a labour of love. The professor is the only copyist to have been allowed to paint the Mona Lisa, so to speak, in the nude — without the protective glass which partially concealed her from the rest of us. Not only are its overall dimensions identical with the original's, but every feature of the painting, every shading and brush-stroke, no matter how minute, has been measured on the original and exactly reproduced. The colours are equally precise. Other copyists use modern compounds. The professor made this copy so as to better understand the chemical dynamics of the original, so as to arrest its deterioration. The pigments and emulsion are the same as those used by Leonardo da Vinci.

'He created this replica over a period of twenty years. The result is a copy which can be distinguished from the original for only two reasons. It is painted on canvas, not wood. And it doesn't have the original's cracklure— the fine cobweb pattern on the surface, caused by the shrinking and cracking of the varnish over centuries, and which is inimitable — as unique to a painting as our thumb-prints are to each of us.'

Six journalists rose to protest. Clavier from *Paris-Jour*, which had staked fifty thousand francs on the uniqueness of the missing Mona Lisa, spoke first. 'That's ridiculous. How do you make a perfect replica of a masterpiece? Leonardo was Europe's greatest genius. Bellini is an academic hack.'

Inspector Charon sighed. 'Next you'll accuse the Pope of not being Christ. Gentlemen, I speak off the record. The public don't like to be told Santa Claus doesn't exist. A painting is not eternal. Few survive well for as long as half the Mona Lisa's age. Some colours fade, others darken, and have to be re-touched. Particles of pigment come loose and drop off, and new ones are substituted. A section will break away from the rest, slip and refuse to be eased back into place. The restorer has to paint it over.'

It was a hot morning and the air in the Press Room was still. Inspector Charon wiped sweat from his cheeks with the back of his hand. 'The Mona Lisa was, or rather is, an unusually sad case. Leonardo dedicated his life above all to experiment. He did not follow the proven paint formulae of his teachers, but devised his own. They were not as good.'

A small man with curly blond hair stood in the back row. 'Ponçolet, *La Vie Culturelle*. So who painted the Mona Lisa that was stolen from the Louvre?'

'Perhaps twenty per cent of it's Leonardo's. The rest is the work of Professor Bellini and his predecessors.'

The silence was broken by Lebrun of *La Dépêche*. 'If it's so close to the original, why isn't the one behind you hung in the Louvre, and the search called off? What difference would it make with the protective glass in front of it? The thief would be left with a near-worthless commodity.'

'Although it's a term not much used in your trade, it's a matter of principle. We're not here to discuss ethics, but the new procedure. From now until the original is recovered, this Press Room will be opened on request any day until eight in the evening. When one of your readers delivers a Mona Lisa to your newspaper, you will no longer pass it on to us. Bring it here, compare it with the professor's replica and only if it resembles it extremely closely ask to see a detective. That concludes this morning's briefing.'

Worth wondered whether he was beginning to share Prefect Lepine's persecutory delusions. If this was a trap, it was one he would have to enter, and leave.

'I've come to pack for you, while you shave and change into these new clothes,' said Angelica.

'Are we going to America?' Perugia was out of bed and fully dressed, but about one-third drunk and smelling of anise. 'Have you brought the money?'

'You're beginning your journey tonight, as far as Florence.' She pulled his cabin trunk from the wardrobe, and found it was packed already. 'He's sent enough money to get you there but no further for the moment.'

'He's got it wrong. Florence isn't on the sea. There's no ships from Florence to New York.'

'There's no mistake. It's where you're going now, for a few days. Paris isn't good for you any more.'

'Have they found out?' His voice was almost apathetic.

'So far, only about your *petite amitié* with Mr Snelling.' She poured water from the jug into the basin, and handed him his shaving brush. 'If you stay, they'll find out more and more. There's no extradition for the offence from Italy.'

He seemed to sober, and started to lather his face. 'I don't much like Mr Snelling since he tried to blackmail me, but he's thoughtful.'

'He's sent you a new passport, so the border police at Modane won't find your name on the list of Louvre employees. And a letter offering you employment in Florence as a restaurant waiter.'

Perugia put down his razor. 'I'm not going to serve in a restaurant to please Mr Snelling. He's obliged to look after me.'

'It's only to show if you're challenged at the frontier. When you get to Florence, his instructions are that you're not to do work of any kind. You're to find comfortable lodgings. Every Tuesday and Friday, at ten o'clock, you're to go to the *poste restante* counter at the PTT on Via Manzoni. He'll telegraph you money and send your next instructions to you there.'

'Do you trust him?' Perugia was putting on the new jacket Angelica had bought for him.

'If I were you, I'd have no choice, except four years in jail for sodomy or worse. The train leaves at 17.40, from Gare de l'Est. Your ticket, money and documents are on the table. Don't talk to strange men.'

'You've been very nice. I've a present for you,' he said. He bent down and pulled from under his bed a small canvas. It was a reproduction of the Mona Lisa, on which he had painted out her face, and painted Angelica's in.

The combined thickness of the layers of congealed gelatin covering Mona Lisa's image was three-tenths of an inch. There wasn't the time to add a safety-margin; and it was enough to keep her in one piece during the surgery, if Worth performed it decisively and with unusual care.

He tautened the 1/16th mm. steel cheese-cutting wire stretched between his gloved hands and applied it to the top left corner, between the underside of the painting and the wood-block mounting. He found the correct purchase and pulled at the wire with his right hand. As it began to cut into her, Mona Lisa protested in a grating baritone. Crumbs of yellowed plaster spilled into the tray.

Although bloodless, the process of freeing a master-painting from its base was, to the uninitiated, as fraught as watching a surgeon making an incision into your mother's abdomen. Worth pulled the wire back with his left hand, a little more sharply.

The operation had been devised and almost perfected over the past thirty years by European art dealers in their back-rooms, to meet the rapacious demand for masterpieces from J.P. Morgan and rival American *nouveaux riches* collectors. Buy a passable 'from the school of' at auction. Have it improved and revarnished by your gallery's retained freelance restorer. Put it in a hot water-oven for thirty hours. Take it to Villa i Tatti for Bernard Berenson to write his unreserved opinion on the back of the mount that it was by the Master himself. His fee was fifty per cent of its consequently enhanced value. You transferred the painting on to another old mount. You stuck a second faked-up 'from the school of' on to the canvas bearing Berenson's signature on its rear. And you had two authenticated European masterworks for a third the price of a genuine one.

The cheese-cutting wire had reached Mona Lisa's forehead. Worth pulled it back and forth diagonally with steady strokes. Probably no picture even begun by Leonardo da Vinci had been treated thus before. So far, the Mona Lisa was surviving the experience with an almost easy grace. However maverick Leonardo's experiments with paints, his base-preparations — described at length in his journal — were those of a conservative and meticulous craftsman.

The cheese wire was now beneath her left eye and approaching the ridge of her nose. Leonardo had been raised in the Tuscan hills, and as an artist had selected his wood-blocks with a countryman's skill. The close-grained rectangle of poplar he had selected for Mona Lisa had survived four centuries far better than the painting, without cracks or splits or warps. He had spent nine days sanding and stone-polishing its surface, until it was smoother than a sheet of Venetian glass. He had given it a coating of resin, and then applied a layer of gesso — a hand-pestled mixture of plaster and size, smoother than talc — through which Worth had now sawed as far as her neck. When the gesso had dried, Leonardo had put on a second coat of resin, and laid on that the painting surface itself — a sheet of fine, densely-woven linen of a thinness and strength far superior to the canvas later generations of painters had been able to acquire. The wire had reached the top right and bottom left diagonals, and the sound it made had deepened. The gelatin was vibrating. Worth slowed his stroke.

As an artist, Leonardo had despised the oil-painters' approach, applying layer upon layer of globs of wet pigment, constantly covering over their mistakes as they went along, until they achieved something near to the effect they had sought, and a surface as irregular and rough as a Tuscan cow-shed's plastered wall. Leonardo never painted over. Only when he saw vividly in his mind the precise toning and image he wanted did he mix his colour and apply it with his brush to the linen. If he made an error, he wiped it off almost immediately and thought again. When he found his mind still to be blocked, he called street musicians and conjurers into his studio, to entertain him until it cleared. Leonard spent much longer on his portrait of Mona Lisa — in between other commissions he hurried through by comparison, to raise quick cash — than on anything else he created. The single layer of paint was microscopically thin — thinner than its covering of varnish. Sandwiched between the gelatin and the sheet of linen, it seemed hardly to notice the wire cutting through the gesso beneath her hands.

The wire cleared the bottom right-hand corner. Worth's right arm was aching, and he flexed and relaxed it to calm the muscles for the next process.

He wrapped the tray and its contents with cambric, binding it tightly with surgical tape. Slowly, he lifted it, reversed it and lowered it on to the flat bench. He pulled off the tapes. Mona Lisa's new career was about to begin. He lifted the tray, and then the wood-block to which she had been attached for four hundred years, leaving her face-down on the gelatin bed. The underside of the painting was pale yellow, the close linen weave still firm to his gentle touch. He gave it a layer of latex emulsion and began to scrape the residue of gesso from the block.

After ten minutes, the latex was tacky. He placed over it the rectangle of stretch-framed canvas which was to be her new base and delicately pressed it home, until the air bubbles were expelled and the adhesion was complete.

He tipped the crumbs of gesso from the tray into a pestle, added pigment of ochre, plaster and size, and pounded it with the mortar. From a tiny bottle, he dripped resin on to the exposed surface of the wood-block, spreading it with the fingers of his other hand.

Angelica found that her urge to steal had subsided. It was

almost half a year since her farewell shoplifting excursion in Belem, at Seymour's Emporium; and her petty thief's tour of London's more opulent haberdasheries now seemed to her to have been a passing quirk. As with contrived briskness she approached the main entrance to the Prefecture, she saw mostly irony in having to steal again the painting they had already stolen. She could no longer evoke in herself the cold excitement she used to feel. It was as though it had been drained from her to make space for her still-growing love for Worth.

He had said that if nothing more went wrong, within a few days the Paris episode in their lives would be completed. Would Worth then find his own desire to steal fulfilled, and settle down into a gentlemanly existence? She was less than sure she wanted that for him.

The guard at the door glanced at her reporter's pass and pointed to her canvas bag. 'Please open it.'

He put his hand inside, and finger-counted the three ersatz Mona Lisas she and Worth had bought in the souvenir shops in Rue de Rivoli.

The guard picked up a key from his desk and gave it to her. 'When you leave, be sure to lock the door after you.'

Mona Lisas abandoned by other journalists remained piled on the Press Room table. Angelica put the canvas bag on top of them. From it, she took out the middle canvas. It was by far the oldest and markedly better than the rest.

Following Worth's instructions, she fought her instinct to shut the Press Room door. She listened for sounds in the corridor and heard silence. She lifted the Bellini replica from the wall, and in its place hung the one in her left hand.

She gave the key back to the guard in the entrance hall. 'I locked the door.'

'Can I check your bag again, miss?'

'Are you worried I might have stolen something?'

He coughed on the half-burnt and extinguished cigarette between his lips as he put his hand into the bag. 'We want to be sure you're not trying to dump a Mona Lisa on us.'

He counted three paintings. 'A lady like you shouldn't be

doing this work. You should find yourself a husband. Excuse me for troubling you, miss.'

Unless fortune abruptly reversed itself, it would take at least a day before anyone at the Prefecture noticed the switch. In that time, at least thirty journalists and perhaps a dozen detectives would have been allowed into the Press Room by themselves.

When it was detected, how was Inspector Charon to admit to the world that France had lost not only the Mona Lisa, but that the only comparison-replica in existence had gone missing from police headquarters? And if he couldn't, how could a search be launched for it?

Peeling the gelatin from the surface of the Louvre Mona Lisa, securely glued to her new base, required the insertion of more linseed oil than Worth had anticipated — over a quarter-pint — but the separation was clean. She lay face-upwards on the darkroom bench beside the Bellini. The twins stared identically into the dim red light.

Worth withdrew the colour filter from the overhead projector. He and Angelica immediately saw the difference between the two. The eyes of the Bellini version were bright and clear. The entire image of the Louvre Mona Lisa was befogged by browned varnish.

He bent down and through the odour of linseed oil caught a faint scent of paraffin. 'The topmost skin's causing the discolouring. A staining agent's been added to it,' he said. 'I daren't try to lift it because the painting's so thin. Bellini had no preservative justification for applying it. He's muddied her face deliberately.'

Angelica said, 'That's criminal.'

'What's a restorer but a legally licensed faker? I never met a talented one at peace with his jealousy towards the artists whose works he keeps alive. And with reason.' Worth reversed the Bellini on to the sheet of 1/700th-density foam rubber. 'As a technician, a man like Bellini has more expertise than an artist like Leonardo ever bothered with.'

Worth began coating the rear of Bellini's canvas with

173

anehedric solvent. It had been developed by the forensic scientists Lepine so despised, as a means of dissolving the fabric on which a bloodstain was lodged, while leaving the plasma-mass intact, as it would Bellini's paintwork. 'What eats at him is that even if his own pictures were hung in a museum, nobody would give them a second glance. He's no perception about the human condition, nothing to say. He's condemned to being a brilliant toucher-up so he's embittered. And he's covertly, very slightly sabotaged the original, to make his own look the better.'

The layer of new gesso on the Leonardo wood block had become tacky. Worth positioned and smoothed down the rectangle of linen, and spread resin over it.

Angelica said, 'It's still a beautiful painting. After all this, it would be a terrible waste if it got into Morgan's hands and was never seen again.'

'He's senile. He's probably forgotten she exists.' Worth picked up the gelatin sheet and laid it on top of the linen. It should transfer perfectly the intricate pattern of cobweb cracks from the museum version. 'But if it goes back to the Louvre, it's not only the dim light and the protective glass that'll prevent people appreciating it. As long as something plausible's inside the frame, they don't much care. It wasn't Leonardo's perception they came to admire, but the money it's worth.'

He picked up the light frame holding the Louvre Mona Lisa and lowered it on to the top rack of a small, cheap, pine packing case. The box already contained, on its lower racks, hand-painted, canvas-mounted reproductions of Rembrandt's Bathsheba, Fra Angelica's Madonna, Quarton's Pietà and Poussin's Inspiration. He replaced the layer of protective covering, closed the lid and slid the catch into place. The label on the lid read: 'The W.H. Smith Limited Edition Masterpiece Collection of Europe's Greatest Paintings.'

Worth wrote on it, 'Best wishes on your birthday.'

At the Gare de l'Est parcels office, he consigned the box, carriage pre-paid, to the Florence parcels depository, to be collected from there on presentation of the weigh-bill.

John Pierpont Morgan was carried in a wheelchair down the steps from his rented carriage attached to the Northern Star express from Cherbourg Harbour, to the red carpet on Platform One of the Gare du Nord. As the Mona Lisa had not been delivered to him, he had to fetch it.

Lord, I'm not asking you for added time in which to fail, only for enough so I can succeed. His negotiations for an extension of his lease of life on earth were meeting with oblique and unencouraging responses from the Heavenly Freeholder. After the SS *Mauretania* sailed from New York, he had discovered that the medical trade had all but written him out of their future cashflow projections. The two young doctors chosen by his chief physician to go with him to Europe had been sent equipped with little more than sedatives and painkillers. During the crossing, it had seemed that they were trying to starve him towards the next world, on a diet of bouillon, eggs and bread. On the fifth day, he had successfully appealed to the captain to be served steak and potatoes, which had made havoc in his intestines but strengthened his spirit.

At least the physicians' prognosis meant that his soul would ascend from the same side of the Atlantic on which he had been born. He would not see an ungrateful USA again. Before his departure, he had received some final, unforgivable blows. Congress was again trying to break up his painstakingly built industrial empire. William Pinkerton had resigned his services before Morgan had got round to firing him. His American wife, living in his house on the Hudson River, attended by his servants, refused to see him. A judge in chambers was considering his American children's affidavit for an order that he was no longer fit to manage his financial affairs and for the appointment of trustees.

'*Oh say, can you see by the dawn's early light . . .*' While the railway police band played *The Star-Spangled Banner* — he hoped it would be the last time he'd hear it — Morgan's eyes wandered around the people on the platform. Unlike his previous visits to Paris and, in obedience with his instructions to the French Ambassador in Washington, both the President and the Prime Minister were absent. They were probably as content as he was to be spared the encounter. The Government had yet to repay its debts to the Morgan banks run up during the previous war with Germany, and resented his terms for a new loan to finance the next.

He had ordered no press interviews. He glared back at the reporters staring at him from behind a barrier. The face of one of them induced an internal spasm beneath his ribcage. Whether it was of distress or excitement, he had no time to discern. He looked up and saw the slender figure of the man he had asked to be sent to meet him bending over him, a white bowler hat clutched in his right hand.

He shook Morgan's limp hand uncertainly, walked silently behind the wheelchair as it was pushed to the horse-drawn state limousine, and stood with a marked lack of deference while Morgan was lifted by two attendants on to the rear seat.

'Obviously I'm honoured,' said Louis Lepine, sounding as thought he did not feel himself to be so. He sat beside the newly exiled King of American Capitalism, as the limousine followed the mounted escort down Rue d'Hauteville, towards the Plaza-Athénée. Morgan had insisted upon there being no other passengers. 'And I was less than surprised that you should ask to meet me. But why did you want me to welcome you to Paris publicly?'

'The thief must read newspapers. Tomorrow, he'll know that the man with the money has arrived and made contact with you. Whatever he wants for her, he can now have. How much does he want?'

'If he does, he hasn't said; and it's against our policy to ask, Mr Morgan.'

'Your policy's namby-pamby, sir. Not at all that of a nation you'd want to back in a war.' The left wheels of the limousine passed over a raised manhole cover. Morgan tilted to the right, and Lepine helped him push himself back into position on the cushions. 'I already told your Ambassador to tell your Prime Minister, whoever he is now. His and your guarantee of immunity from prosecution and my cash, up to five million dollars. Once the offer's made and accepted, the war-loan's automatic from the day you start shooting Germans.'

'Mr Caillaux asked me to tell you his Government's most grateful, but deeply disturbed by the condition attached. The Mona Lisa doesn't belong to the cabinet. It's state property.'

'There's no bettering the deal. You French are devious, but you can see for yourself the condition I am in. France can count on getting nothing for its war from my successors. Did my nurse give your driver my menthol-pads?'

Lepine looked in the small bag which had been placed between them and found one for him.

Morgan applied it to his huge nostrils. 'It'll only be for a few months that I need the painting. Then it will revert to France, in perpetuity and at no cost. If you don't obey . . .'

His voice trailed away as he returned the menthol-pad to his face.

'You are a very important man, Mr Morgan. But France is not the United States of America.'

Morgan inhaled again. Was Prefect Lepine, too, trying to taunt him into the grave? His breath steadied, and his mind cleared. 'That fellow at the railway station. How long have you had him following me?'

'I'm responsible, partly, for your life while you're here. I've had a detachment of plainclothes guards around you since you landed in Cherbourg this morning. Has one of them disturbed you? Could you recognise his face?'

'I never had a memory for faces, thank God. That's your kind of job. It was the way he looked at me.'

'Can you describe it?'

'No, sir.' Morgan was staring through the side window.

'When have you seen it, him before?'

'A while ago, standing outside my mansion in New York. And, I think, from a taxi cab.'

Lepine signalled to the chauffeur, but not discreetly enough.

'What've you told him?'

'To drive more slowly.' They were a third of the way along Boulevard Haussmann. 'If you want the painting recovered, perhaps you're not telling me as much as you should. Understand that this limousine is all that I can slow down. When did you decide you needed the Mona Lisa?'

Morgan leant back on the cushions. 'I was once approached by a fellow called Adam Worth. He asked me for a lot of money, saying that he'd steal the Mona Lisa for me. I sent him packing, and sent Pinkerton after him. He went to London and killed himself in a sewer. Mr Lepine, I came all this way to meet you because he told me you were the world's finest detective. Now damned well prove it to me. When you do, there's an extra million dollars in it, in trust for your children.'

Lepine said, 'I've no children, nor a wife. I'm a public official.'

Morgan had fallen into a doze, but woke momentarily. 'If only I had been born without testicles. What I could have achieved.'

The canvas had dissolved completely after the second application of Anehedryde. With a block of manicurist's pumice, Worth erased the minute indents it had left on the back of the painting. He gently rolled a cylinder of modelling-clay over it to remove the powdered debris, and brushed on a coat of resin.

The Leonardo wood-block was ready. He lowered it on to the Bellini replica, allowing its own weight to impress the pattern of cracklure. His hands on the top and bottom edges of the wood-block, he lifted the picture from its foam-rubber mattress and turned it over. To the eye, at least, the adhesion was flawless. He placed it beneath the 450-watt heating element. Torpidly, minutely, the glutinous varnish cracked and curled, following the lines of the tiny ridges in the gesso beneath.

After twenty minutes, he turned off the heat and eased away the globules of resin from the join between the picture and the wood-block with a surgical scalpel.

The resin was not quite dry. He sifted Parisian dust from a salt-shaker around the sides of the painting, and carried it into the natural light of the salon.

The result was perfect enough to convince any expert but Bellini.

'My shot, I think,' said Louis Lepine, his back turned as he studied the cues in his rack. 'As you see, I have had my servants leave the two balls exactly as they were when we had to interrupt the game.'

Looking at the table, Worth saw that the black had been moved diagonally a couple of inches, to the first player's advantage.

Lepine aimed and shot the white ball towards the black, which sped in the direction of the left-centre pocket and missed it. 'My skills are deserting me. After this frame with you, I'll be giving up snooker.'

Worth took an angle with his cue. Both men could see it to be a bad one. 'You've decided you prefer chess?'

'Just over two hours ago, I gave my resignation to the Prime Minister.'

Worth hit the black ball gently sideways, so that it rolled into the D. 'You decided to let the thief win?'

Lepine picked up a cold chicken leg from the buffet-table. 'He'll feel that he has when he reads the papers tomorrow. The journalists won't dare explain it was political.'

He wiped his hand on a napkin and picked up his cue. 'Mr Caillaux told me that, given my failure thus far, I must make a public statement guaranteeing the criminal immunity from prosecution, in return for the painting.'

He struck very hard with his cue, ricocheting both balls between the cushions. 'So that's that.'

'Did you remonstrate?'

'You're quite new to France and the way we work. Two members of the cabinet have dismissed themselves already over the Mona Lisa, to keep the National Assembly at bay. If I'd stood up against the Prime Minister, he'd have had to resign.'

A pocketing shot was still impossible. Worth repositioned the black near the centre of the table. 'What will you do now? Retire to your vineyard in Algeria?'

'I'll go abroad for a while, certainly.' Lepine cued off, and missed.

'Wouldn't that be a breach of contract between us?' said Worth. 'We have an agreement for a series of articles called Europe's Master Detective.'

'I'll offer your agency first rights in my autobiography, though I fear there's only two or three people who'll understand it. Meanwhile, I'll leave you to finish the game for me while I go upstairs and pack.'

As Lepine walked from the room, Worth looked at the table. It would have taken a single, straight shot to pot black.

The Court Page of *The Times* of London, published daily except Sunday, was more than a reprint of the last circular from Buckingham Palace, naming those King George and Queen Mary had received in audience, and which lords and ladies were in waiting. It was the social noticeboard for those who ruled Britain, closely read by many more who did not.

Money could not buy the transference of an announcement of a birth, christening, engagement, marriage, death or funeral from the classified advertisements to the Court Page, alongside the guest-lists of regimental dinners, diplomatic receptions, Grand Lodge ladies' nights (His Majesty was a Freemason) and boarding-school speechdays.

On Wednesday, two brief items on the Court Page were separated by three columns. The French Ambassador had given a private lunch at his residence for Mr L.S. Lepine, lately Prefect of Paris, attended by the Home Secretary, the Rt. Hon. Winston Churchill and the Commissioner of Scotland Yard, Sir George Winterton.

Those intending to attend interments in Highgate Cemetery

on Thursday morning were to note that it was to be closed between ten and midday by order of the Metropolitan Police, and all burial services would be held two hours later than had been advertised.

'With all the talk of a German invasion, there's recently been great demand for our long-distance tourers,' said the English salesman in the Bentley automobile showroom on the Champs-Elysées. 'The only one we have left is our demonstration model. We won't be importing any new stock until the diplomatic situation is clarified.'

If one has to leave a country without being noticed, the most prudent disguise can be ostentation. Angelica glanced at the shiny, dark green, gold-trimmed machine. 'I'll take it.'

'Very good, madame. I'll note down some details. Then I shall have the vehicle prepared and sent round to you next week.'

'I'll take it now.'

The Englishman tried hard not to shake his head. 'That will hardly be possible. It takes the bank four days to clear the cheque. Then there's the special driving instruction. A Bentley is not a Ford or a Renault. Will you be driving her yourself?'

'My chauffeur is outside with gold sovereigns. He does not speak English. Please take from him only the exact amount, and give him the key.'

The salesman paused as he was closing the passenger door behind her. 'Would it be impertinent to ask whom I have had the honour of serving?'

'Deeply so,' said Angelica, taking the door handle.

The salesman bowed. Worth, in chauffeur's livery bought that morning, saluted him, started the engine and drove into the traffic. It was eleven o'clock. It would take the Home Office pathologists in London until mid-afternoon to establish that the body from the Highgate grave could not be Worth's. The Paris police, when they entered the apartment, would find his and Angelica's personal possessions in place, and on the table in the dining room a cold lunch waiting, of coddled quail eggs, poached salmon with watercress sauce and a bottle of good Pouilly-Fumé.

The Belgian border was three hours away.

14

November in Flórence, squatting on the flat valley of the Arno between the Tuscan hills, was low cloud and drizzle. During the three hours the Uffizi Palace remained open to the public on four days a week, you could roam among the Medici's gaudy treasures and hardly meet another foreigner, or a Florentine.

The tourists would return in April. Many of the shops of the narrow, damp, windless streets of the birthplace of the European Renaissance were closed for the winter. Many of its citizens had little occupation but to enquire at the post office whether a relative had remitted money from abroad.

As a hotel, the Albergo della Republica on Via Manzoni had few merits, except that it was open out of season and had a corner suite with an uninterrupted view of the entrance to the Central Post and Telegraph Building on the other side of the street. On Tuesday morning, at fifteen minutes past ten, Vincenzo Perugia went in.

He came out again into the rain, petulantly crumpling a note in his right hand. He crossed to the hotel.

'Did you expect me and Francesco to wait around for you in this Italian dump for ever?' He had refused Worth's offer of the only armchair, whose back had a head-level grease patch and whose sides were in need of darning. 'I've become more than sick of living here on thousand-lire-a-week handouts. The agent says studio space in Bronx is fast selling out. Where's our steamship tickets and our money? I've more than earned them.'

'It's now one step away from you,' said Worth.

Angelica said, 'Mr Snelling's had some difficult procedural

problems to resolve. Most particularly, finding where you left the painting.'

She picked the heavy, brown-paper-covered parcel from the sidetable and offered it to him.

Perugia stepped backwards on to the frayed rug. 'If you don't want it, why should I? It's dangerous. That's not New York, it's the penal colony.'

Worth said, 'It would quickly become so if you do not do with it precisely as we tell you. No more, no less.'

'Sir, I already know what I'm going to do with it. Which is to leave it here.'

'You've found other arrangements for your and Francesco's passages?' Angelica asked.

Perugia was silent.

Worth said, 'Take it to the Uffizi, now, before it closes. Tell the man at the desk you have to deliver the package personally, by hand, to Professor Dr Enrico Bellini.'

'What if the professor won't see me?'

'He will if you let the concierge feel the package. When Bellini opens it in his office, he will ask you how you got it and why you brought it to him. You'll reply in exactly these words, "I seek no financial reward, only honour. I was a menial Italian labourer in the Louvre, haunted by the fact that France has pillaged Italy of so much of its noblest art. One morning in August, I became so incensed that I stole the Mona Lisa. I now return her to Italy, where she belongs."'

'If I was Bellini, I'd not believe it.'

'It's a well-drafted police statement,' said Worth, closing the window against the rain. 'It'll read even better in tomorrow's newspapers. You're about to be a national hero.'

'I hate Italy as much as Leonardo da Vinci did. I'm going to take your parcel and claim the rewards.'

Worth spoke to him softly. 'You've already been bought two cabin-class passages from Genoa, a studio near Central Park in New York, and there's ten thousand dollars waiting for you in the Morgan Bank on Fifth Avenue. Ask Bellini or anyone else for a reward for the Mona Lisa and you immediately turn yourself into a criminal who can be sentenced to forty years, in Italy or France. You took the painting because you are an Italian patriot. You can't be extradited. The maximum sentence is six months with one fifth remission for good conduct. Your studio's waiting. Repeat after me. I seek no financial reward, only honour . . .'

The crowd of Florentines in the Piazza del Duomo did not seem to notice the drizzle. As the prisoner was led from the police van, they cheered and then a chant rippled through them, growing louder and louder, 'Perugia! Perugia! We love you, Perugia!'

The escorting *carabiniere* released the handcuffs and paused to allow him to acknowledge the tribute. Perugia smiled and waved, then mounted the steps to the courtroom.

Professor Bellini's struggle with his conscience, if one had taken place, had been brief. After less than half an hour, he had pronounced his painting to be without question Leonardo's. Inspector Charon and Dr Desgard, the Louvre's curator of pictures, had arrived from Paris the next morning. They had conferred with Bellini, examined the work of art for themselves. On the back of the wood-block, Desgard found the secret identification marks whose existence had been known hitherto only to him. Charon announced that the Mona Lisa had been saved for civilisation. As France's gesture of thanks to the Italian authorities and people, she would be on display for a month in the Uffizi, then at the Villa Medici in Rome, before being ceremonially returned to the Louvre.

At first, on finding himself in a police cell, Perugia had sulked. Then the presents began to arrive: roasted wild pigeons, smoked hams, tortellini in cream, baskets of apples, chianti and spumanti, an emerald-encrusted pendant of St Anthony, envelopes containing money and proposals of marriage. After a few days, the door of his cell had been unlocked, to allow him to receive his admirers personally, in the police station lobby.

Perugia entered the dock of the court. The jury, as well as the spectators in the public gallery, rose respectfully to their feet. The charge was read by the prosecutor. Perugia pleaded guilty.

The presiding judge asked, 'Is there anything you wish to say to the Court?'

Perugia pulled himself upright. 'I am proud to be found guilty of striving for the honour of our Motherland. Long live Italy! Long live the Italian people! Long live our Italian genius!'

The jury broke into applause. The presiding judge said, 'Under the penal code, the minimum sentence I am allowed to pass is six months. Allowing for the time you have already been confined, and for remission for good conduct, you will be a free man in twelve weeks. I shall instruct the governor to accord you special privileges. God go with you.'

'Mr Worth.'

Worth and Angelica turned and saw the small, white bowler-hatted figure of Lepine hurrying towards them across the piazza. 'Please come with me to the police station. And madame.'

Worth looked round the square and saw two routes of escape. He stood where he was and smiled gravely. 'Our name isn't Worth. This isn't France. You've resigned.'

'You misunderstand. If I asked my colleagues here to arrest you as the real thief, they'd probably throw me inside for slandering their new national hero. I want only to borrow their equipment to take your left thumb-print. A souvenir.'

Worth did not believe him, but it would be inexpedient to run. He pointed to the other side of the square. 'Go over there to the toy shop. Buy a junior detective's outfit. In ten minutes, you'll find us in Café Bruno.'

'My only pleasure now,' said Lepine, pressing Worth's thumb on to the pad of carbon grease between the glasses on the marble tabletop, 'is seeing you both wondering whether you've won.'

He lifted Worth's thumb and raised it above a folded white paper napkin. Worth twitched at the moment of convergence. It was so light, Lepine noticed nothing until he peered at the impression through his junior detective's magnifying lens, and saw the smudge. He shrugged. 'A junior criminal's response to a junior detective's kit. If only even now I understood you better. After all these months, our contest ends as it began on

the day you stole the painting. Your victory's been in con-
triving to beat me by about four hours. If only I hadn't been
such a perfectionist as to have you disinterred before arresting
you. If only the pathologists hadn't been so Englishly pains-
taking. If only the Paris police hadn't sat waiting for you to
return to lunch. If only I'd told them to watch the car showrooms for a lady cash customer with a manservant, instead of
the railway stations for a man or a couple. If only I'd come
directly to Florence. If, if, if.'

Worth drank Punt-è-Mes while Lepine thought, It's for the
best. Perugia's so unimpressive, the theft itself will be forgotten
in a year or two. You'll not get yourself into the history books
as the first international master-criminal. As with the best
punishments, yours is self-administered. He crumpled the
paper napkin into the ashtray and set light to it with a match
from Worth's box. 'That smudged left thumb-print is the only
proof of Adam Worth's existence. I swore a written statement
for the President of the Court that the one on the picture frame
was Perugia's. To protect the situation I've had the evidence
removed from the Prefecture's files to my personal archives.
The corpse has been reinterred at Highgate with suitable
prayers and no change of name. I must report to you that your
widow's taste in gravestones is both vulgar and parsimonious.'

Worth was about to speak, but Angelica broke in, 'What's
the punishment? You talk as though you're giving us a licence
to go wherever we want, to do whatever we want. I don't
believe you.'

'You're right.' He waved away the smoke from the napkin
smouldering in the ashtray. 'Your husband's one of those
criminals who finds moral consolation in assaulting property-
rights and not people, unless you regard Morgan as one. He
needs much more than money to motivate him. He's stolen the
world's most valuable object, partly to prove he was Adam
Worth, a man of surpassing ingenuity and imagination, and
not just another overreaching Litvak from a slum near
Boston. What he and I have proved together is that he's
neither.'

'So who is he?' Angelica asked.

'An ingenious figment of his own imagination. And with

what future challenge, other than to abolish his unhealthy cigar-smoking and to polish his snooker-play?'

'You're a cold bastard,' Angelica said.

'Many women have made similar remarks. My illegitimacy was the work of my parents. The coldness took time to acquire. Although you yourself don't know your husband as deeply as you wish, you're deeply in love with him. The war that's fast approaching is going to be a terrible one — so terrible America will have to intervene, and on our side, to stop France and Germany destroying one another entirely. On my way here, I sent a Marconi-gram outlining your husband's qualifications for special service to my friend in Washington, Alfred Pelaw.'

'Worth alone. That's to be my punishment,' Angelica said. 'And you think it's quits. If you've resigned, why are you doing this?'

'It's an official resignation. The Prime Minister ordered me to play along with J.P. Morgan, to secure a government loan. I can't resign my vocation.'

Lepine sighed, 'I never cared much personally for the Mona Lisa. Long before we were born, it'd lost the original brilliance Leonardo put into it. The Bellini's good enough to go behind the glass in the Louvre. What I can't forgive is that you sold out to Morgan's greed.'

The little grocery store in the side-street in the artisan district on the wrong side of the river Arno had recently gone bankrupt, and been cleared of its stocks of food. The sign on the window, hand-scrawled from behind in mirror writing, announced, 'THE PERFECT GIFT FOR 1ST COMMUNION, NUPTIAL, CONDOLENCE. 99 MONA LISAS MUST BE SOLD.'

Worth said to Lepine, 'I traded Leonardo's and four hundred lire for the best of theirs. He demanded the surcharge because mine was the more faded and cracked. He'll ask you two thousand lire, but you can beat him down to fifteen hundred.'

When Lepine reappeared, he said, 'He sold it to an apprentice art-restorer and his fiancée for a thousand. What did you do with the one you swapped it for?'

'Had it delivered to J.P. Morgan at his hotel. What do you intend to do now?'

Lepine tugged at the sleeves of his jacket in an attempt to straighten the crumples. 'I'll go back to Paris, write my life story and lock it in a bank-vault.'

After the race by private train through France, and the voyage on the chartered steam-yacht across the Mediterranean, and the ambulance journey from Genoa, the royal suite of the Excelsior seemed to Morgan as good a place as any, except that he'd forgotten why he'd come and some damn fool had hung a picture of a girl above his bed. He no longer needed to be held down on to the mattress by the restraining-straps. He stopped breathing.

His mind and senses lingered on in his inert, now painless body and heard the doctors pronounce him dead.

'What shall we put down as the cause?' one asked the other.

'We'd best ask New York. With such a great man, it might cause a lot of upset to tell the truth.'

Morgan's brain fought to move his whitening lips, but could not. 'Put this down, you young fools,' he shouted inwardly. 'Cause of death: self-disgust.'

Then he felt remarkably coherent and calm. It was not the distressing experience he had anticipated. He was entering a tunnel. He was being pulled from behind, so could not see where it ended, or if there was light there.

One Mona Lisa hung above the mantel in a terraced cottage on the outskirts of Florence, looking down at the sofa on which a couple, half-undressed, made love. A garland of wild flowers was lodged in the bride's black, straight, long hair.

One Mona Lisa went to the Louvre. Germany invaded France. Prime Minister Caillaux was tried and convicted for having been a secret agent of the Kaiser. His wife, Lepine's confidante, shot with a revolver in the street the editor of *Le Figaro*, who had acquired her extra-marital love letters and announced his intention of publishing them. She was sent to a separate prison. Lepine did not re-enter public life. Snelling went back to Cincinnati and set up as a consultant in art security. On his release from prison, Perugia decided to remain in Italy, where he and Francesco opened a shop dealing in artists' materials.

Angelica went to the house Worth had bought in New Hampshire, with a pasture on which cows grazed, sloping down to a lake where perch jumped. Soon after she discovered she was pregnant, she received a telegram from Mr Pelaw in Washington saying that Worth had given his life for the allied cause on a heroic mission in Montenegro. It was Easter Sunday. She had not gone to church. The day's brief warmth was rising like an invisible blanket. She put another log in the stove, wondering where Worth was, hoping to hear from him soon.

ABOUT THE AUTHOR

Martin Page trained as a reporter on the *Manchester Guardian,* and after serving in the *London Daily Express* Paris bureau, became a war correspondent in Algeria, Borneo, and Vietnam. He served as the *Express*'s Moscow bureau chief and then its diplomatic correspondent before moving into the magazine field. Page's first thriller, *The Pilate Plot,* was selected Best First Novel of the Year by the British Arts Council in 1979. Page and his wife divide their time between London and New Hampshire.